Alyxandra Harvey-Fitzhenry

waking

ORCA BOOK PUBLISHERS

Library and Archives Canada Cataloguing in Publication

Harvey-Fitzhenry, Alyxandra, 1974-
Waking / Alyxandra Harvey-Fitzhenry.

ISBN 1-55143-489-X

I. Title.

PS8615.A766W34 2006   jC813'.6   C2005-907811-1

Summary: Haunted by her mother's death and struggling against an
overprotective father, Beauty has lost her desire to be an artist.
Then she meets Luna and everything begins to change.

First published in the United States, 2006
Library of Congress Control Number: 2005938905

Orca Book Publishers gratefully acknowledges the support for its publishing
programs provided by the following agencies: the Government of Canada
through the Book Publishing Industry Development Program (BPIDP), the
Canada Council for the Arts, and the British Columbia Arts Council.

Cover design: Lynn O'Rourke
Cover photography: Getty Images

Orca Book Publishers   Orca Book Publishers
Box 5686, Stn. B   PO Box 468
Victoria, BC Canada   Custer, WA USA
V8R 6S4   98240-0468

Printed and bound in Canada

09 08 07 06 • 5 4 3 2 1

For my parents, who have always encouraged me to keep writing and never once tried to convince me to work in an office, thereby saving both me and said office.

For Jess, who always wants to read more. "Picture this..."

And for my husband Khayman, because he woke me up when I hadn't even realized I was asleep.

⊷— PROLOGUE —⊷

THIS DREAM IS NEW.

For months now I've been dreaming of my mother lying in the old claw-foot bathtub my dad tore out of the bathroom after the accident. *I wish I'd known. I wish I'd paid more attention. But this isn't like the other dreams; this one is something else entirely. I still wonder, though, what's the use of dreaming true, of sleeping stories that really happen, if I can't prevent them? If only I'd said something, anything.*

But I didn't.

That must be why I'm here now, quiet and dead inside, and in a new place. This isn't my bed. It's not even my room, with the fading wallpaper and the smell of roses. This is someplace entirely different, a forest at twilight with dark trees poking bare branches into the indigo sky. It's stark here and cold.

The stars are far away and the moon is touching someone else tonight. The only sound is the wind and dry leaves crunching under my feet.

I wish I was alone, but I'm not. She's here, in her black black dress with its long beaded train, watching me, following me. The Shadow Lady.

And I'm lost.

THE SUN WAS PALE BEHIND
the birch trees. It wouldn't be long before the air filled with
yellow leaves. Beauty knelt in her garden, her back to the
road, her eyes full of roses. They climbed the low stone wall,
curled around the painted trellises and gathered on either
side of the steps. Soon they would cover the front door.

She remembered how her mother used to spend long
Sunday afternoons in the garden, picking roses to leave
all over the house and sneak into Beauty's lunch bags. The
petals fell on the grass and stuck to the windows when it
rained. It always smelled like summer in the house.

After *the accident*, as her father called it, Beauty was the
only one left to care for the garden. Her dad knew nothing

about flowers and didn't have the time, anyway. But she loved it, loved the feel of cold wet dirt and the ladybugs that landed on her hands. It made her feel closer to her mother somehow, made her remember the good things.

Her mother had planted the first rosebush, red as raspberries, shortly after Beauty was born. It was still blooming, under one of the windows, reaching tall leggy stems out to find the sun. It was nearly lost in the wild jungle of roses Beauty had chosen mostly for their names: *The Fairy, Dream Weaver, La Belle Sultane, Legend* and *Blue Girl*. She remembered picking them out of her mother's seed catalogs every winter when she was young and then planting her own roses when she was old enough to help out. These days she often sat in her room when it was dark and repeated the names to herself over and over again like some Tibetan chant.

She wiped her forehead, pushing her long hair back. It touched the ground when she leaned over to pick some nightshade. The vines choked her roses if she let them. The sound of footsteps on the stone path leading up to the house distracted her. She turned and shaded her eyes from the sudden glare of light. A long shadow stretched over the ground and touched her. She blinked.

"Hi," Luna said.

Luna was the New Girl and would probably still be known as the New Girl when they graduated in two years.

Briar High was like that. She grinned around a lollipop that smelled like watermelon. Her short blond hair stood up in its customary spikes, dusted with glitter and the odd pink streak. It was as if she didn't even know she was named after the moon and burned just as brightly in the darkness.

Beauty smiled at her even though she suddenly felt plain as a dandelion with her boring hair and lip gloss.

Luna surveyed the flowers, her eyes widening. "Wow," she said. "Impressive."

Beauty stripped off her gloves. "Thanks."

"Did you do this all yourself?" Luna asked, stepping up to run a finger over the unfurled petals of an *English Garden* rose the color of apricots. There were freckles on her nose.

Beauty nodded. "My mom taught me. She planted most of it, but I've been adding a lot."

Beauty and Luna shared a few classes, but they'd never really talked. It had barely been a month since school had started up again. Beauty wouldn't have thought Luna even knew where she lived. Everyone knew where Luna lived, though—in the old Victorian house on Thorntree Avenue. It was painted indigo and rust and lavender. All of the younger kids in the neighborhood said it was haunted and dared each other to ring the doorbell on Halloween.

Luna bent to smell the flower. She didn't settle for a discreet sniff but instead buried her entire nose right into its center. "I love picking them," she said, "but it seems so sad to kill them just so I can look at them for a day."

Beauty shrugged. "The plants grow bigger the next summer when you cut them back a little." She snapped off the stem of the rose and handed it to Luna. Something about the other girl made her bold and nervous and relaxed all at the same time. She felt like it might rain, suddenly and without warning.

Luna grinned, tucked it behind her ear. Beauty counted seven earrings. Her father wouldn't even let her get a single set of holes in her ears. It just wasn't fair.

"Thanks," Luna said around the chunk of candy in her mouth. "Listen, I dropped by to talk about our English project."

Beauty nodded. She'd nearly forgotten. Mr. Kingsley had paired them up. Having to work with a partner was bad enough, and she still wasn't entirely certain how she felt about being put with the New Girl. It could have been worse, though, much worse. She could have been put with Poe, and then she would have drooled all over her chin and not thought of a single intelligent thing to say. He just did that to her.

She recalled a vague rumor that he'd been out with Luna once or twice, but that they weren't seeing each other anymore. She decided to pretend she hadn't remembered that.

Besides, Luna had already dated a couple of other guys since then. And it wasn't like Poe even knew Beauty existed.

"Kingsley didn't really give us a topic," she said instead. "He said to pick a literary movement or something, right?"

Luna nodded. "Yeah, he seems pretty nice. Any ideas?"

Beauty shook her head. "Not really."

"We could do it on the Pre-Raphaelites."

Beauty blinked. "Who?"

"They were this totally cool bunch of artists and poets who did all this stuff using myths and fairy tales."

"Oh. Okay, sure."

"Great. My mom's an artist and our house is *so* Pre-Raphaelite it's ridiculous. It'll be easy to do research. Too bad we couldn't do a tour or something as our project."

Beauty thought of the unfinished paintings in the basement. "Your mom's an artist?" Her tone sounded wistful, even to her own ears.

Luna shrugged. "Yeah. We usually have artists and writers and musicians staying with us. No ghosts yet, though, which sucks. Why don't you come over this week and we can start researching?"

"Okay."

"Cool." She reached into the pocket of her jean jacket. The fringe of beads around the edge jingled softly. "I have something for you."

Beauty frowned. "For me? Why?"

Luna shrugged. "I don't know, why not? Here." She handed her a brooch with a pale carving of a hand holding a rose on it. The lines of the carving were narrow and delicate, every fingernail and petal sharply delineated. The edge was ruffled, as if the arm was clothed in an old-fashioned lace sleeve. "It just seems like something you should have."

"Thanks." She didn't know what else to say. She felt like giggling but didn't want to seem totally uncool. She wasn't used to people just giving her things; most people barely knew how to talk to her anymore.

"It's a reproduction of Victorian mourning jewelry." Luna wiggled her eyebrows. The left one had a small silver hoop through it. "That doesn't creep you out, does it?"

Beauty shook her head, ran a thumb over the carving. The last of the sun caught the silver pin, flashed like water. Her father would freak out if he saw it. She slipped it into her gardening glove. It was the easiest way to sneak it into the house.

"Are you sure?" she asked. People didn't just give gifts to girls they barely knew. It was weird, but she loved it. She was suddenly glad there was a New Girl.

Luna nodded, grinned again. "If there's one thing I've learned it's that girls with weird names have to stick together."

AFTER DINNER WAS FINISHED and the dishes loaded into the dishwasher, Beauty took her cup of rosehip tea outside onto the back porch. It was still mild out and the stars were just beginning to glitter in the sky. Her dad was puttering around in his workshop. He'd been working on a new cabinet for the kitchen since last Christmas.

She lit the candles she'd stuck in old jam jars and tilted her head back, waiting. The moon was slowly creeping over the tops of the houses and there was a moth behind her, slamming into the screen door. Crickets called to each other in the bushes. It wouldn't be long now.

She'd learned the routine during the summer, had caught on by the end of June. She was glad her father liked to fiddle about with hammers and saws on Sunday evenings, because she liked nothing more than to sit in the warm night air and listen, just listen.

She heard a back door slam a few houses away. The neighbor's sprinkler system clicked on and water fell like dew into the leaves of the old maple by the fence. Over the steady sound of the dripping trees, she could hear the brush of fingers on guitar strings and a dark voice filling the space between her and a long-haired boy.

Poe sang, as he sang every Sunday night, alone in his backyard. He didn't know his voice carried to a long-haired girl drinking tea and dreaming. His eyes were closed, and he didn't hear the raccoon on the roof or the cats fighting across the street or even his own heartbeat. He only heard the music in his head, pouring out like wine from a fallen goblet.

Beauty knew he didn't know she could hear him, barely knew they even lived on the same street. She was too shy to say anything, too convinced he would laugh at her or, worse, ignore her completely. Too convinced he would be afraid of her.

Better to be quiet, to be another shadow at dusk listening to him sing.

She drank her tea and his honey-dark voice. She wondered what he would think if he knew how it made her feel. Like she was alone and not alone, like there was nothing between her and the trees, like she was a candle burning, like she was rain falling from a pink sky. She could forget there was a desert inside her.

She flipped open her tiny sketchpad, the one that was small enough to fit into the back pocket of her jeans, and found a blank page and a pencil. She drew softly, letting images travel from his song to her paper. She sketched his hands, long and callused, and felt herself blushing. She wondered if Luna had just walked up to him and introduced herself, had dared him to take her out. Or maybe he'd waited for her one morning outside math class or slipped a note into her locker.

The tip of her pencil snapped, pockmarking the paper. She was getting carried away. She couldn't help the small sigh when she heard him slip into The Doors' "Waiting for the Sun." Ever since school had started up again, she'd dreamt of him kissing her and this song playing all around them. His dark hair tickled her cheek and his hand settled on her knee. The memory of it made her shiver and blush and made her feel like hiding.

She barely heard the screen door slide open behind her.

"Beauty, telephone!"

Her dad's voice might have been lightning slicing into a tree. She expected to see sparks and smell smoke. Her name seemed to echo. Poe's song ended, and she knew, with breathtaking humiliation, that he had heard her name bellowed over his singing and had stopped. The knowledge was like an ice cube dropped down the back of her shirt on a hot summer day.

Her chair scraped the flagstones as she pushed to her feet and ran inside.

NIGHT WAS THICK OUTSIDE her window. The streetlights and the blue glow of television screens flickering along the street were not comforting. The scrape of tree branches against the side of the house was like a raspy breath.

Beauty hated this time of the night, when everything was quiet and her homework was done and there was nothing left but to get into bed and try to sleep. It was like a medieval dungeon of comforter and cotton. She remembered when she used to tuck herself in under the sheets and snuggle into her pillow and pretend that the sun wasn't sliding warm hands over the window and spilling out onto her bare floor. She'd close her eyes and remember her dreams and smile.

That was before her mother died. Morning was her friend now, dawn the prince's kiss.

"Good night, sweetheart," her father said, poking his head into her room. He wore his customary blue bathrobe, the one that was fraying and older than she was.

She smiled at him.

"Night, Dad."

"Sweet dreams."

She held the smile in place until he closed her door softly behind him and his footsteps echoed down the hallway. Sweet dreams. As if.

She sighed. She couldn't put it off any longer. She slid into the bed, took a deep breath and shut off her lamp. The wind moved the trees outside her window, making a shifting pattern like lace falling over her face. The smell of roses was strong.

She knew her father would be asleep before his head even hit the pillow. She'd be able to hear him snoring in a few minutes. Sleep was never a problem for him because he never remembered his dreams.

She pulled the blanket up over her face and tried not to think about it. It was a useless effort since it was all she could think about every night. Her dreams were always vivid and a little odd, but the ones that had a creepy habit of coming true were usually about tests or missing the bus to school. Her mother claimed it was a gift that the women in her family carried in their blood. She remembered her mother's mother telling of the time she woke in the night from a dream of fire just before a candle tipped and sent her curtains up in flames.

The only dream Beauty remembered now was one too bright and too sharp: her mother in a bathtub of rose petals in the garden with dark red corsages on each wrist.

And the woman in black watching her.

— 2 —

MONDAYS SUCKED.

There was no way around it. Beauty peeled the plastic wrap off her sandwich and wondered if bologna and cheese on white bread constituted child abuse. Beside her, Sabrina sucked ginger ale through a straw and then grinned.

"Bologna and cheese?" asked Sabrina.

Beauty rolled her eyes. "How'd you guess?"

"It's Monday, isn't it? You always get bologna and cheese. I still don't get why you don't just buy your lunch like everyone else." Sabrina poked at the congealing pasta on her paper plate. "Not that this mess is any better."

Beauty tossed her sandwich aside and picked up the apple instead. She knew without looking that her lunch bag also held raisins and a granola bar.

"You know my dad," said Beauty. "He's afraid the cutlery's dirty and I'll accidentally fall onto a plastic knife and take out my spleen."

Sabrina shook her head. Her dark hair was cut into a smooth chin-length bob with white-blond streaks. Her eyes were dark and faintly exotic, a gift from her East Indian mother. Beauty had always admired Sabrina's features; they were so much more interesting than her own.

"No offense, Beauty, but your dad is getting weirder."

"I know." Beauty felt herself shutting down again, felt the distance stretch between her and her voice. She'd known Sabrina since kindergarten, and they'd been friends through unfortunate growth spurts and even more unfortunate pimples the size of quarters. Sabrina had come to the funeral, and her mom had made piles of warm chapatis because she knew Beauty loved them so much. It was a comfort to have a friend who had known her for years, before everything seemed to unravel. Even so, it wasn't enough to bridge the gap that she felt growing between her and everyone else, between her and herself. Sometimes she wished no one knew her and she could be the New Girl and start from scratch.

"Do you still have to shave your legs in the gym bathroom?" Sabrina asked.

"Yeah," Beauty sighed. "No razors allowed in the house. He keeps his locked up in his medicine cabinet."

Sabrina shook her head. She would have said more, but Beauty was getting that lost sorrowful look again. She tore open her packet of cookies and pushed one over.

"Here, have a chocolate cookie. Guaranteed to solve all of life's problems."

They chewed in silence for a while. Beauty turned when she heard laughter and the tinny sound of an acoustic guitar. Poe sat in the back corner with some of his friends. His long hair was tied back, and he was wearing a leather necklace with some kind of pendant on it.

Sabrina nudged her under the table. "Go make a request."

"Yeah, right," Beauty scoffed. "I told you what happened last night. I request that he forget me altogether."

"You are way too shy. Go sit in his lap."

Beauty's laugh was slightly strangled, like a bird suddenly free of a cage and afraid of the sky. "Go get your head checked," she suggested.

Sabrina just laughed. "You know you want to."

"I want a lot of things."

"Good," she said with a nod of her head. "It's a start." She wadded up her wrapper and flicked it off the table. It bounced off a black steel-toed boot.

Luna kicked the wrapper aside and slid onto the bench beside Sabrina. She was wearing a skirt over faded patched jeans and a long medieval velvet shirt and yellow nail polish. Nothing about her remotely matched.

"Can I sit here?" Luna asked. There was a bindi in the middle of her forehead and faded henna on her palms. She wore thick silver on her fingers and a candy ring. The girls at the table next to them nudged each other and sneered. "I'm Luna," she said to Sabrina.

Sabrina smiled. "I know. I'm Sabrina."

"Hi." Luna pulled a bag of popcorn out of her knapsack. The smell of movie theaters and summer afternoons was thick and sudden. She shrugged. "No food in the house," she offered by way of explanation.

"Wish we had that problem," Beauty muttered.

The girls at the next table laughed. Luna ignored them. One of the girls leaned over, all false smiles, and stared pointedly at her. "You know, Halloween's not for a month," she said sweetly.

Luna ignored her. Sabrina blinked innocently.

"Then you might want to consider wearing a paper bag on your head until then," said Sabrina.

There was a shocked gasp. Luna made an odd sound as she tried to swallow a giggle.

"Thanks," Luna said finally, offering her popcorn. "I don't even know her."

Sabrina shrugged. "That's Clare. You're not missing much. She was, however, going out with Matt Doran in August."

Luna winced. "I went to the movies with him a couple of weeks ago."

"I know."

"I haven't seen him since," she continued, defending herself. "He was boring. There are definitely more interesting guys around here."

"It doesn't matter."

Luna sighed. "I really hate new schools sometimes. I wish they came with a manual."

Sabrina brushed salt off her hands and grabbed her bag. "You're doing fine. I gotta go." She made a face at Beauty. "See you in language lab."

Luna watched her go. "She seems nice."

Beauty nodded. "Some people are scared of her, though."

"Why?"

"She's never been one to take any crap." Beauty shrugged. "Some people are scared of me too."

Luna opened a bottle of pineapple juice. "Really? How come? You're so quiet."

Beauty rested her chin on her hands. "They think I'm weird. You haven't heard the stories yet?"

Luna shook her head. "Nope. Do you have an evil twin or a secret life as an adolescent marketing spy?"

"Nothing that interesting. Don't worry, I'm sure you'll hear all sorts of things soon enough."

Before Luna could reply, Poe walked by their table and paused. He was carrying his guitar case, and the earphones around his neck blared out unidentifiable muffled music. His friends Kennedy and Paul didn't notice his abrupt pause and stumbled into him.

"Hey, Luna," Poe said, his ears pink. He glanced at Beauty. "Beauty, right?"

She was suddenly absolutely certain there was a huge piece of her lunch stuck in her teeth. And that her entire knowledge of the English language had escaped her completely. Sometimes she hated her life. She realized he was still looking at her and she hadn't said anything yet.

"Right," she whispered, nodding. "Hi." *Brilliant. Just brilliant. I've probably got drool running down my chin too. Oh my God, does he even know how beautiful he is? I have to get out of here.*

Luna smiled. "What's up?"

He shrugged. "Not much. Finished that song."

"Cool. You'll have to let me hear it later."

"Sure." He smiled at them both. "See ya around."

Beauty waited a full minute before speaking. Her stomach felt weird and her throat was dry. She watched him saunter away, guitar case bumping against his leg. He didn't look back.

"Is he...are you together?" she blurted out finally. As she waited for Luna's answer, she was uncomfortably aware of every sound: the crinkling of paper, laughter and whispering, a shout, a book being dropped and the blood moving in her veins. It shouldn't matter what the answer was. She knew Poe would never look twice at her. He was so...and she was...well, she just wasn't. It was as simple as that. And he must know about her and her mother. Everyone knew, it seemed, except Luna.

Luna shook her head. Her blond hair was sleeked down today and it made her look like a disoriented flapper. "Nah, we thought about it but we make much better friends."

It was as if all the air had left Beauty's body and then a wind had stormed into her. She knew her smile must have been too bright, too obvious. She almost didn't care. "Oh. You went out though?"

"Sure. I've been out with a lot of people. It's how you make friends."

Beauty wondered how it must feel to be so confident and casual, so natural. "Most people aren't like that around here," she said.

Luna glanced ruefully at Matt's ex-girlfriend. "Apparently." She shook her shoulders as if to shake off the whole situation. "Anyway, who cares? Why don't you come over later? We can talk about the project. I have an idea."

Beauty tried to follow the abrupt change of topic. Half

of her was still swooning over the fact that Poe had said her name. Sad. She really had to get a grip.

"Beauty?"

"What? Oh, sorry. Sure."

Luna grabbed her bag and slung it over her shoulder. It was covered with beads and patches, and the back was painted with a woman in a rowboat looking tragic.

"Do you need directions? It's right near your place."

Beauty had to smile. "Everyone knows where you live, Luna."

Luna grinned. "Ah, I'm famous already."

"You have no idea."

BEAUTY SPENT HER SPARE period before math class in the art room. It was mostly empty; one or two students she didn't know were talking over wet clay in the far corner. The old radio was playing something instrumental that sounded vaguely like a waltz. Mr. Andrews only stocked classical and jazz CDs. Anything else students wanted to listen to they had to bring in themselves. Mr. Andrews was a very popular teacher. He wore jeans and he was only ever strict if you didn't take care of the paintbrushes properly.

Beauty took a deep breath of the paint-and-turpentine-laced air. It was strangely comforting. She loved the old and stained tables and the rickety easels and the canvases that hung in every available space to dry. Baskets of charcoal and pastels shared space with tubes of paint and glue and brushes of every size and description.

She stood in front of her easel and pursed her lips. Her sketch was off somehow; something was missing and she didn't know what it was. The woman had her mother's features, and the bathtub was just an outline. The garden was rendered in painstaking detail, every rose opening and every petal sharply shaded. But it was flat, dull. Anyone could have drawn it; it had no character.

She sighed and reached for a palette and paints. She'd try adding some color and see what happened. It couldn't get much worse than it already was.

She painted slowly and quietly for awhile. It made her uncomfortable to be in the classroom where anyone might come in to watch her. She preferred painting in her basement where she knew she was alone and could wear paint-splattered shirts and thick black eyeliner. At school she tried to fade, tried to make everyone forget all of the stories about her. She just wanted to be invisible. Except when she wanted to shoot through the halls like a falling star.

Luna had had a taste of Briar High this afternoon. It hadn't taken long for people to figure out that she didn't exactly fit in. And fitting in was practically an Olympic sport at their school. Lately, Beauty had started wearing vaguely trendy clothes so she could blend, so no one would remember that she didn't fit in either. She still half-expected someone to stand up in the middle of a biology test and scream "freak!"

She'd never been able to decide if her gravestone would read "She tried too hard" or "She didn't try hard enough."

But Luna, Luna wasn't even trying. She lived in an old house everyone thought was haunted. Her mother had purple streaks in her hair and a nose ring, and Luna swam naked in backyard pools, even when they weren't hers. The guys from school all watched her through the fences and gates and from treetops. If it had been anyone else, they'd have hooted and hollered. Instead they just watched her silently, staring at her plump body as if it held some kind of answer. Once someone had even stolen roses from Beauty's garden and left them in the pool's sharp waters after she'd gone.

Guys didn't watch Beauty at all. Well, except when she tripped over her shoelaces or froze in the middle of a class presentation. Lately her idea of rebellion was chewing gum in class. She was about as dangerous as tea at four in the afternoon with your deaf grandmother. If Luna was a firefly, then Beauty was the glass jar.

She snorted to herself. Luna might be a glass jar too, if she had Beauty's father. Sabrina had it right: Her father was getting weirder. She knew he loved her, but he was becoming so overprotective it was ridiculous. They both knew her mother's birthday was soon, the first one since *the accident*. It made Beauty tired and numb inside, but it seemed to be doing the opposite to her father. He was nervous and edgy.

She shook it off and turned back to her painting. The acrylic was drying quickly and she knew without a doubt that it was no better than the black and white sketch. She ran her hands over her face and turned away. She tossed her paintbrush aside and her eye caught the glint of an X-Acto knife lying among the ruins of a newspaper that had been used for papier-mâché.

She picked it up, the yellow plastic handle as hot as fire in her palm. The blade was short and slanted like a guillotine. She looked at the canvas again and then at the forbidden edge of the blade. When she sliced it across the canvas, it parted the paint like water. The edges of the canvas curled to the wooden frame on which it was stapled. She sliced at it until it hung in tatters like a bead curtain. Strips of paint and material fluttered down to drape over her hands like the long petals of pale lilies.

When the bell rang, she jumped and the knife nicked the base of her thumb. Drops of blood formed and fell, red as rose petals. The pain was quick and sudden, and it felt like a tiny mouth breathed on her hand. She stuck it between her lips and sucked at the blood, feeling a little bit disoriented and a little foolish. She turned her back on the ruined painting.

Her father would freak out if he saw the cut on her thumb. She wrapped it in a wet paper towel and hurried off to class, wondering how she was going to hide it from him.

─ 3 ─

THE DAY WAS STILL BRIGHT
and warm when Beauty walked up the driveway to 17
Thorntree Drive. The tall house was a riot of muted colors
and the gardens were a wild mess. She itched to get in there
and start pulling at the weeds. The black-eyed Susans were
choking and the roses were growing leggy, stretching out
to search for sunlight. Wind chimes, Chinese fortune coins
and tin lanterns danced in the maple tree in the front yard.
Somewhere down the street a dog barked.

She paused in front of the lavender-hued door and lifted
the brass knocker shaped like the snake-haired face of
Medusa. She jumped when the door swung open suddenly.

A barefoot woman in a sundress barely glanced at her. She was concentrating on the old book in her left hand, and her fingers were stained with ink. Her hair hung down to her elbows.

"Yeah?" the woman asked.

Beauty hesitated. "I'm, uh, looking for Luna?"

The woman nodded, waved her in. "She's around," she said before wandering off.

Beauty stood uncertainly in the front hall. The living room was off to her left and the walls were crammed with paintings, mostly of women in medieval gowns or knights in armor. The lamps were off, fringed shades like ornate Edwardian hats. She could see dusty plants in the kitchen, and the hallway was papered with intricate dizzying patterns in burgundy and green. The air smelled like burning wood and paint.

Luna laughed from the top of the staircase. It was old and wooden with a faded carpet runner marching up the center. She was barefoot too, and silver rings gleamed on her painted toes. A jumble of Indian anklets rang out when she crouched down to be seen.

"Never mind Simone," she said. "She gets like that when she's writing poetry."

"Is she your sister?" Beauty asked.

Luna shook her head. "She just lives with us sometimes. Come on up."

Beauty climbed the stairs, feeling like she was entering Aladdin's cave or some distant land where oranges grew in rivers and flowers were eaten for breakfast. Luna led her down a narrow hallway. Doors opened onto several rooms filled with easels and towers of books. They went up another staircase and Luna ducked into the door on her left. A purple bead curtain swayed and clinked together, sounding like raindrops on the roof.

Beauty's eyes widened. "Wow," she said. "You've got a great room."

Luna grinned and threw herself down on her unmade bed. "We move around a lot. I've learned to decorate quickly."

There were candles burning on the windowsills and incense smoke coiling lazily from a wooden holder shaped like a branch. Music she didn't recognize spilled out of a small stereo covered in rhinestones and star stickers. The sound of it was thick with drums and women's voices, making her think of long nights and abandoned castles. There was a desk and a chair and a beanbag cushion surrounded by a pile of embroidered pillows. Beauty lowered herself down into one and had to smile. She felt dangerous and interesting and her name suddenly didn't seem so absurd.

Posters of rock bands and movies shared space with reproductions of old paintings. Beauty recognized the sad woman painted on Luna's knapsack.

"Who's that?" she asked.

Luna followed her gaze. "The Lady of Shalott," she replied. "She was cursed never to look on Camelot, but she saw Lancelot in her mirror and fell in love with him. When she turned to look at him, she saw Camelot and died in the river."

Beauty tilted her head. "Cheerful."

Luna smiled. "I like it. Tennyson wrote a poem about her, and that painting's a Waterhouse. He was a Pre-Raphaelite, like the guys I told you about."

Beauty nodded. She felt oddly comfortable around Luna, as if they'd been friends for years. It seemed perfectly normal to be sitting around chatting about dead artists. Luna pointed to a pile of books on the low blue table between them.

"I pulled out some of my mom's books on the Pre-Raphaelites. You can borrow a couple if you want." Beauty picked up the one on top and flipped idly through it while Luna kept talking. "The Pre-Raphaelites revolutionized art in the mid 1800s. They used these really bright colors and they painted on white canvases instead of the traditional black ones. It was a big deal. They were like a rock band, you know? Everyone talked about them. Am I boring you? I tend to babble when it comes to this stuff. It runs in the blood."

"Is your mom really an artist?" Beauty asked wistfully.

"Yeah, half the people living here are artists or poets or musicians. It's very much a Pre-Raphaelite house. Even Poe and some of his friends have been by to rehearse. The basement's soundproof, for all the musicians to practice in if it's late. My mom's weird about getting her eight hours of undisturbed sleep. Anyway, where was I? The project. Right. So that's why I thought we should do that as our topic. Kind of cheating, but why not? What about your mom?"

It was like the air filled with dust.

"My mom worked in an office building. She loved her gardens, though."

"What happened?"

"She died." Beauty picked up another book and forced a smile. "Does your mom have a studio here?"

Luna watched her for a moment but decided not to push it. "Yeah, I'll show it to you later if you want."

Beauty thought of her cramped corner in the basement with virtually no light and paintings stacked under the couch, and then she thought of a real artist's studio.

"I'd love to see it," she said. It was the first thing she could remember wanting this much since her mother died. Well, except for Poe. And she just liked watching him.

"You're an artist too," Luna said decisively. Beauty looked up, startled. It was something she normally tried to hide.

Artists didn't last long at Briar High, and she was sick of being talked about.

"What makes you say that?" she asked suspiciously.

Luna shrugged. "I'm either wildly psychic or I noticed the paint spots on your shoes. Your choice." She grinned. "I'd go with wildly psychic. It's much more romantic."

"Oh." Beauty smiled, told herself to relax.

"What happened to your thumb?"

Beauty's hand clenched as she glanced at the thin red cut. Her shoulders tensed. "Little accident with an X-Acto knife," she whispered. It was a small cut but slightly inflamed. Her dad would notice it in a second. "My dad'll freak," she said, mostly to herself.

Luna sat up. "Why? It's tiny. I had to have stitches once when I decided it might be cool to juggle steak knives like I saw at a carnival." She winced. "A very bad idea. I bled everywhere. Star completely lost it."

"Star?"

"My mom. I've never seen her so twitchy before." She shrugged. "Anyway, I have an ugly scar, and I still get a weekly lecture on being careful and it's been nearly six years. Parents are so weird."

Beauty could just imagine what her father would do with a story like that. He'd have a heart attack, simple as that. "My dad's a little…overprotective."

Luna nodded. "Must be nice."

"Where's your dad?"

Luna shrugged, tried to look indifferent. "We don't know. Anyway, you can hide that cut, you know."

Beauty put the book down. "Really? How?"

"I have just the thing." Luna pulled a wooden jewelry box off a table draped in silvery scarves and rummaged through a staggering jumble of necklaces and brooches and earrings. "It's in here somewhere...a-ha! Knew I still had it." She pulled out a wide silver ring and tossed it into Beauty's lap. "Just wear it on your thumb. It'll hide the cut."

Beauty felt slightly nervous, the way she always did when things seemed to be going too well. She slipped the ring on and the cut disappeared.

"Perfect," Beauty said. When she looked up, she was grinning. "Thanks. But you already gave me a brooch for no reason."

"So, borrow the ring until the cut heals. No big deal."

Beauty wanted to hug her but she worried it might be weird. Instead she tried to remember why she was here in the first place. "So, what was your idea?"

"Well," Luna said, gesturing wildly with her hands, the way she always did when she was excited, "the Pre-Raphaelite Brotherhood, or the PRB, had a journal for a while. It was called 'The Germ,' I think. Something like that. Anyway, it didn't last long, but I thought it might be fun if we put a journal together. You know, with poems and art and a couple of essay-type things so Kingsley doesn't think we're just slacking off." She stood up and began to pace through the room. "You could do the art since you draw. I can only draw stick people," she continued, ignoring Beauty's little sound of protest. "And we could make copies for the whole class. What do you think?"

Beauty nodded slowly. "Could be fun. I don't know about my drawing, though. You've never even seen my stuff. You might think I suck."

Luna waved her hand dismissively. "I'm sure you're fabulous. Better than me anyway. There wouldn't be that much to do; most of the paintings would be photocopies of PRB stuff, anyhow. Is it a deal?"

Her enthusiasm was infectious. Beauty nodded, barely worrying if Mr. Kingsley would think it was a good idea or if they should ask him about it first.

"I'm in," she said firmly. There was a release, like a melting river in spring, bursting suddenly free of its banks. She flopped back in the beanbag. "How do you like Briar so far?"

Luna snorted and began to juggle three small rubber balls. "Are you kidding? It's high school. What's to like?"

Beauty snorted too. "I thought you were more optimistic."

Luna laughed. "My mother's the happy-go-lucky hippie; I just play one on TV." She shrugged, nearly dropped a ball. "That's not really true. It's just a pain sometimes going from school to school and from town to town. And the rules are always different."

Beauty stared up at the glow-in-the-dark stars on the ceiling. "I don't know, I think we're pretty typical. High school wouldn't be a rite of passage if it didn't suck."

"True." Luna let the balls fall and roll under her bed. "But why are those girls so uptight? It's like they think I'm going to steal all of their boyfriends or something."

Beauty raised an eyebrow. "You have been out with a lot of guys since you got here. Any juicy details?"

Luna tossed a sock at her. "No. It's not like that. I just don't really believe in monogamy."

"You don't?"

Luna shrugged. "Not really. I hate the whole jealousy thing. It makes people do stupid things. But regardless, I was only trying to make friends. I've always had more guy friends than girl friends."

"Well, Clare and her friends would rather you cower in fear when they walk the hallways. It's their thing."

Luna made a face. "Not going to happen. Who does she think she is, Marie Antoinette?"

Beauty laughed. "You say the weirdest things."

"Guilty. I was homeschooled for a long time before this current rotation of schools."

"Was it hard?"

"I loved it. I just decided I wanted to meet more people my age." She stopped, folded her arms with a wicked, troublemaking smirk. "Can I ask you a question?"

Beauty groaned. "I smell danger."

"Maybe. You like Poe, don't you?"

Beauty shot up into a sitting position and stared at her like a deer caught in headlights. "No!" she said quickly.

Luna lifted her eyebrows. "I won't tell, I promise."

"I barely know him." It wasn't a lie exactly.

"What if I tell you a secret in return?"

Beauty chewed on her lower lip and then squinted as if she were caught in a horror movie. "Okay. You first."

"I have a crush on Kennedy."

Beauty watched her start to pace again. "Really?"

Luna nodded. "I got it bad, girl. He's just so…cool."

"Kennedy? Long blond dreads, chatty, so laid-back he might as well be a rug?"

Luna giggled. "The very one. Does he have a girlfriend?"

Beauty shook her head. "If you're going to fall for a guy at Briar, he's probably your best choice. He's nice."

"Think he'll go out with me?"

"Have you been turned down yet?"

Luna stuck out her tongue. "Ha, ha." She rolled her shoulders back. "Wow, that feels better. Your turn."

Beauty swallowed. "Uh."

"You promised. Now spill it."

"There's nothing to spill," she said finally. "You have no idea how boring my life is."

Luna rubbed her hands together. "I can fix that."

Beauty groaned. "Just let me lust from afar." She shuddered. "This feels weird. Isn't he like your ex or something?"

Luna rolled her eyes. "I told you I don't work that way. Besides, we're just friends. Although he is a great kisser." She burst out laughing. "Beauty, you're bright red."

Beauty tried to stop herself from blushing but with little success. She sighed. "He's so yummy."

Luna nodded. "He is that. You should talk to him."

Beauty stood up, pushed her hair back. "Please, one life-altering moment a day." She felt suddenly jumpy and jittery, like she wanted to twirl in circles all day. It was the happiest she'd felt in months. She glanced at her watch. "I've got to get home; I'm late for dinner."

Luna followed her down the stairs to the front door. Piano music trailed after them from one of the back rooms. Luna rolled her eyes when the singing started, high and loud and just a little off.

"Beauty?" Luna asked, leaning against the door.

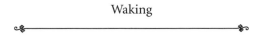

"Yeah?"

"I'm glad you came over."

Beauty smiled, touched the Victorian mourning brooch on her jean jacket. "Me too."

— 4 —

I'M ON A PATH, IN FRONT
of a small cottage. The gardens are wild and full of roses, some
blooming and fat, some withering on their stems. The sun rises
slowly in a wash of lilac and orange. Night falls away behind
me, and the stars wink in the indigo sky. I smell wood smoke and
wine and something sweeter, like sugar burning.

The stones under my feet are wet and lead up to the cottage.
With its thatched roof and stone walls, it's like something out
of a fairy tale. Frogs croak as I make my way up the path. My
breath hangs in the air. I'm wearing a simple long dress woven
of ruby-hued linen, and my hair is loose down my back.

Candles burn behind the diamond-paned windows. I go to
knock on the door, but it creaks open before I can touch it.

"Hello?" I call out tentatively. This is the point in all those horror movies when you think the heroine is stupid for going down into the basement or into the abandoned shack. I know if I was watching myself right now, I'd be throwing popcorn at the screen. But movies just don't convey the stubborn need to be strong or the curiosity I feel.

I know if Luna were here she'd waltz through the door and make herself at home. She'd probably even rearrange the furniture.

That thought is all the encouragement I need. I'm sick of myself and dreaming seems to be the only way I can be someone else.

I walk through the open doorway and pause in the welcoming heat. The walls are whitewashed and plain, the fireplace carved of polished oak. Candles glow on the mantelpiece and a fire pops on the hearth. More candles burn on every available surface: slim raspberry-colored tapers in plain holders and silver candelabras, fat red pillars in clay bowls or on plates, and votives flicker like stars in a stream. Roses grow inside the cottage, creeping up the walls and winding around the windowsills. The tiny red buds, held in tiny perfect green-leaf hands, wait for the breath of summer.

I'm alone in the cinnamon-scented room, but it feels kind of like dawn is holding its breath all around me. It's like everything is frozen, a moment captured in perfect winter, even though there's no snow and the air is soft. I wonder who lives here and why everything is so quiet, so still.

The only furnishings inside are a hope chest painted red, a rocking chair and what looks like an old-fashioned spinning wheel next to a basket of red wool. I shiver when I notice it, but I don't know why. I approach the spinning wheel slowly, the way one might reach out a trembling hand to a strange dog. My heart stutters and my mouth goes dry.

I wonder why I feel as if I have no control over my surroundings. I keep drifting toward the spinning wheel as if I'm a ghost on water or mist blown through a field.

I stretch out my hand, pale and long-fingered, the red red cut at the base of my thumb, red as petals, red as berries, red as pomegranates.

I'm a breath away from the wheel and the spindle. The rocking chair creaks behind me. My heart pauses, then resumes its beat with a vengeance. A red bird exploding in my chest.

"We're not supposed to touch that," a small voice says.

I jump and whirl around, yelping. I press my hand to my chest, try to keep my heart under its cage of flesh and bone. Some things just aren't meant to see the night. I notice the tiny cut has opened again and is weeping blood. It's the same color as my dress.

A little girl sits on the edge of the chair, swinging her legs. She's wearing shiny black patent leather Mary Janes and a red dress. Her dark hair is in two long braids and tied with satin ribbons. I remember those ribbons well. They'd been my treasure the summer I was seven. The shoes always pinched my toes. I'd hated wearing them.

I have to concentrate on my breathing before I can say anything.

"Why not?" I ask.

The girl shrugs. "Don't know. Not supposed to, that's all." Her eyes widen. "You're bleeding."

I look at my hand, then hide it behind my back. "I'm okay," I tell her.

"It makes Daddy sad."

I bite my lip. "Sometimes."

The girl keeps swinging her feet even as she pulls out a small jar and a wire wand. She blows bubbles into the warm air. They float and twirl like fairy mirrors. They make me smile.

"Do you live here?" I ask her.

The little girl shrugs again. "Sometimes."

"Where do you sleep?"

"I don't like sleeping. I'd rather play." She blows more bubbles, laughing when they burst over the candles in a shower like frost.

I turn back to the wheel.

She leaps off her chair and spins around in circles, still filling the air with bubbles. "Play with me!" she says. Her laugh is like cotton candy. I find myself laughing as well and spinning with my arms stretched out like branches. The room blurs around me and looks like a field of wild poppies. When I'm dizzy and out of breath I stumble to a stop. I'm still grinning. The cottage is a cottage again.

The little girl tilts her head and looks at me. "Dreams aren't supposed to hurt."

I blink. "What do you mean?"

"We didn't know, did we?" Her lower lip sticks out as she pouts. The jar of soap drops out of her hand and rolls across the rag carpet. "It's not our fault."

Her eyes are huge and wet. I shake my head and try to answer through the narrowing and burning in my throat.

"Dreams aren't real." It's the only thing I can think to say. It's what I'd always wished someone would say to me when I had nightmares. Instead, I remembered them and worried if they would come true.

"But we saw her in the bathtub in the garden. It's not fair," she wails, stomping her feet.

"It's not your fault," I tell her firmly.

She stops abruptly, sniffles once. "Really?"

"Really."

"Really and truly?"

I nod. The little girl smiles brightly and climbs back onto the chair, rocking and swinging her feet. The bubbles stay afloat, like pollen.

"Okay."

I'm not sure if I want to laugh or cry. I turn back to the spinning wheel with its rungs tied with red ribbons. The wood is polished and smooth. It looks soft as butter. Baskets of wool grow at my feet like berries. I ignore the creaking of the rocking chair. I touch the wheel and hold my breath, tensing. When nothing happens, I laugh a little and spin the wheel. The ribbons tangle in the air. The wood sings as it moves. Firelight flickers and dances, shooting sparks into the chimney.

The edge of one of the rungs catches the tip of my forefinger, taking a delicate bite. I stuff the finger in my mouth, blood tasting like old pennies.

The little girl cries out. "She's here," she says, voice trembling.

I can make out a shape on the other side of the window. "The Shadow Lady," I whisper. I'm cold all over.

"She's going to hurt us."

I shake my head. "I won't let her," I promise.

The Shadow Lady moves away. The wheel stops and when I turn back to the rocking chair, it's motionless and empty. I'm completely alone in the cottage.

I look at my finger, bleeding and raw. There's a slim pale splinter under my skin, digging in like teeth, like the tip of a knife. Blood drips onto the floor. As it falls it shimmers and turns to roses, red and full, petals unfurling like fingers. They gather at my feet, thickening like a lake around my ankles and up my calves. Thorns snag my dress, tearing at the fabric. The roses are growing frantically along the walls and across the floor, reaching out for me as if I'm the sun.

I wake up when petals begin to fill my mouth.

— 5 —

BEAUTY WOKE TO THE
TASTE of petals in her mouth and the cloying scent of
roses on her pillow. She scrambled out of bed, heart ham-
mering as if she was being chased. She pushed her tangled
hair back and cursed when she caught a glimpse of her
alarm clock. She'd slept through the annoying buzzer and
wouldn't have time for a shower. She kicked the corner of
her bed to make herself feel better, but only managed to
stub her toe.

She fished out a long skirt that was crumpled in the back
of her closet and threw on a tank top and her jean jacket.
She twisted her hair back, stuck a couple of lacquered chop-
sticks through it and decided that was all the attention it

was going to get. When she looked in the mirror she was pleasantly surprised to see she didn't really look like herself. It was a start.

She raced down the stairs and nearly collided with her father in the kitchen doorway.

"Morning, honey," he said, kissing her cheek. He was wearing his favorite pair of faded jeans and a denim work shirt. She knew the tool belt wouldn't be far away. She'd babysat for months to earn the money to buy it for him for his last birthday. And even when he was home from working at the hardware store, he still liked to putter around and fix things. "I was about to come and get you. Are you feeling okay?"

She poked her head into the fridge and rummaged for the juice.

"I slept through my alarm," she explained. She tried not to snap at him. She was still feeling raw from her nightmare, but that was no reason to take it out on him. The dream felt as if it was thick in the air. She could still hear the creaking of the rocking chair, the crackling of the fire. And the blood.

"I made you some toast," he said, nodding toward the table. A plate piled high with buttered toast sat next to a bowl of sliced apples and melon. She picked up the perfectly cut fruit.

"Dad, I could have done that myself," she said, struggling to keep her voice even and mature. "I'm not a little girl anymore."

He didn't look at her, instead fiddled with his tool belt, attaching it so it hung properly. "We've talked about this, honey."

She rolled her eyes.

"You've talked, Dad, and I've had to listen. That's not exactly the same thing." She wanted to make him understand, but she didn't know what else to say. He never wanted to talk about it. It was easier for him; he felt comforted, safe. She was the one who had to sneak into the locker room to shave her legs. She was the one who hadn't had her hair cut since it happened. She wasn't even allowed to work at her embroidery loom or make her own dinner anymore.

Her dad looked up.

"It's just safer this way," he said. "You could have an accident or hurt yourself."

"I'm not her," she said quietly. The words seemed to hang in the air like knives. When he didn't say anything, she sighed. Hugo Dubois was every bit as stubborn as his daughter. "Dad, I'm sixteen. I think I can handle it."

"We'll talk about this later."

"No!" She said, slamming her glass down so the orange juice sloshed over the top. "You always say that."

"Beauty."

She knew that tone well. She clenched her teeth together to keep herself from screaming. He wouldn't even look at her now, had stopped listening. She recited the names of roses, *Nearly Wild, Gingersnap, Fortune-teller*, until she was calm enough not to throw her glass at the wall. "Fine," she snapped instead. She grabbed her knapsack and pushed past him. There was no point in talking to him anyway.

"Aren't you going to have any breakfast?"

"I'm not hungry," she yelled before storming out of the house.

SABRINA LOOKED AT BEAUTY. She was leaning against her locker with her arms crossed and an expression of sulky anger on her face. Her hair was coming out of its knot, strands falling into her eyes. Sabrina winced.

"That bad?" she asked, taking her math book out of her locker. She was secretly glad that Beauty was worked up over something. She'd been too calm and uncaring for too long.

Beauty kept staring into the crowded hallway. The noise was swelling as classes let out for lunch. Someone's bag hit her shoulder, but she barely moved.

"You actually yelled at your dad?" Sabrina continued. She'd never even known Beauty to snap at her father. She was too calm for that, too scared to say anything.

"Yeah."

"Cheer up," Sabrina said. "Everyone fights with their parents. That's what they're there for."

Beauty sighed. "I don't."

Sabrina raised an eyebrow. "I know. It's not natural."

"I guess. He's just been so weird lately...since *the accident*." Her mouth twisted bitterly. "It's like he's afraid it's in the blood or it's contagious or something."

"He's just worried about you."

"I know," she said. "I'm drowning in it."

Sabrina shut her locker door and propped one shoulder up against it. "Do you want me to ask my mom to talk to him or something?"

Beauty half-smiled and shook her head. "I don't think that would help, but thanks."

Luna poked her head around the corner and grinned. "Who needs help?" she demanded.

Sabrina snorted. "You do, apparently. Are you aware that you have several hundred butterfly clips on your head?"

Luna twirled once, laughing. She was wearing a leather jacket with a secondhand bubble-gum pink prom skirt. She plucked a barrette from her hair and attached it to Sabrina's streaked hair.

"So, what were we talking about?" she asked.

Sabrina glanced at Beauty. "Beauty had a fight with her dad."

Luna tilted her head. "My mom goes all creepy quiet when she's mad at me," she said. "What does your dad do?"

"Walks away." Beauty bit hard on the inside of her mouth when her lower lip started to quiver. She would *not* cry. She hadn't cried since before her mom's funeral and she wasn't about to start now. Not here, in the hallway, in the middle of the day.

Luna slung an arm over her shoulder and gave her a quick hug. Beauty couldn't remember the last time someone at school had done that. For a long time people just seemed afraid to touch her, even talk to her.

"Wanna call him names?" Luna asked brightly. "It always helps me."

Beauty shook her head. She knew her friends were just trying to help, but they would never understand. Since her mother's death, she and her dad had only had each other. It felt wrong to fight with him, dangerous. What if something happened to him before they made up again?

Beauty felt the tears burning at the back of her eyes. She hated feeling like this, all angry and guilty and scared. "Never mind," she said. "Let's not talk about it anymore, okay?"

Luna nodded. Beauty and Sabrina followed her to her locker. Luna ignored Clare and her friend, who sneered from across the hallway. They'd been doing that for a week now. Clare just didn't seem to understand that Luna didn't care about Matt and didn't have the same ideas about dating as she did.

What she couldn't ignore, though, was the state of her locker.

The word "slut" had been scrawled across the door. Luna swallowed, shut her eyes briefly. Some schools were harder than others, she told herself. It didn't matter what strangers thought, even if she prided herself on never having met a stranger. She liked to think everyone was a friend she hadn't met yet.

But sometimes it didn't work that way.

Clare and her friend burst into laughter. Sabrina whirled around and glared at them. She was about to say something when Luna shook her head.

"Don't," Luna said quietly. "You'll give her power over me if you acknowledge her."

Sabrina's mouth tightened. "Hard for her to have power if I sit on her and make her eat glue."

Luna smiled, but Beauty could see the sadness behind the curve of lips. She knew the feeling all too well.

Luna gathered her binders. The inside of her locker was covered with photocopies of Pre-Raphaelite art and a small painting of a woman at a banquet with Luna's mother's signature on the side. She closed her locker, snapped the lock shut and refused to look at the graffiti.

Something unfurled inside Beauty. She, unlike her father, was starting to learn that some things shouldn't be ignored. She dropped her knapsack on the floor and dug through her stuff until she found a bottle of blue paint and a brush.

"Just a minute," she said firmly.

Luna and Sabrina watched her curiously. When Luna looked at Sabrina, she just shrugged. Bored, Clare and her friends walked away.

With her paintbrush in hand and a tube of sky blue acrylic paint, Beauty felt powerful, in control. It was like a shawl settling over her shoulders, and she loved it. She wasn't sure she'd ever felt like this before. She'd definitely never been this public about her art before.

Her strokes were quick, slightly hesitant, but the image that took shape on the locker door was fluid and pretty. The butterfly had curved wings and a woman's body, and it covered the vandalism completely.

"Oh, Beauty," Luna said. "It's beautiful."

Beauty shrugged, suddenly embarrassed. She could feel the speculative eyes of the students walking by. She tried not to blush.

Luna stared at the butterfly a little longer before glancing past Beauty's shoulder and lifting her hand in a wave. "Hey, Poe. Come here."

Beauty's eyes widened instantly. Sabrina tried not to laugh at her terrified expression.

"What are you doing?" Beauty hissed. "I thought you liked the painting."

"This is my way of thanking you," Luna whispered back, barely moving her lips.

"Why? Do you hate me?"

Luna giggled but didn't say anything else as Poe sauntered up to them, knapsack over his shoulder. His hair was down, falling into his face. He was wearing old cargo pants and a black T-shirt, and his Discman was in his pocket, as usual. Beauty felt her mouth go dry.

"Hey," he said. "What's up?"

"Not much. I wanted to remind you that I can't sing for the band after school. I have to work on a project at Beauty's house." Luna glanced sideways at Beauty. "Right?"

Beauty nodded. "Right."

Poe shrugged. "Okay. We'll do it later."

"Sure," Luna agreed. She grabbed Sabrina's hand. "Okay, we gotta go. Bye," she said before they hurried down the hall toward the cafeteria.

Beauty wasn't sure if she wanted to run after them, hug them or kill them. She was horribly aware of her mouth. She wanted to smile but was afraid it would look like a grimace or that he'd think she was nauseous. Which she suddenly was.

She couldn't think of a single thing to say.

He just stood there, way too gorgeous, with his battered-up guitar case, flicking his hair out of his eyes. The silence stretched on. She was feeling desperate and terrified that she would start stammering about the weather or current events.

Someone just shoot me now, she thought. *Put me out of my misery. He's going to think I'm some kind of an idiot. I'm not ready for this sort of thing.*

Poe saw the wet paintbrush in her hand and looked at the butterfly gleaming on Luna's locker. "Did you paint that?"

She nodded. "Yeah, just now," she added in a rush. "Someone wrote on her locker."

"I'll just bet they did." His jaw clenched. "People can be such jerks. What did it say?"

She told him, anger burning the back of her throat all over again. Poe shook his head and swore. She tried not to be distracted by the way his eyes glittered.

"I don't think this school is ready for Luna," Beauty said, slipping her free hand into her pocket.

Poe glanced at her, smiled slowly. "You seem to be doing okay," he remarked.

Beauty shrugged. "I like her," she said. "I guess you do too." She stopped, wondered if it was too late to bite her tongue right off. Why had she said that? Why was she reminding him that he'd dated her and that Luna was way funkier and prettier and cooler than Beauty could ever hope to be? She really *was* an idiot.

Poe glanced at her. "She's like a sister," he said. "I hate to see people down on her."

Beauty felt like grinning. Luna had already mentioned that she and Poe were better off as friends, but it was much nicer hearing it from him. She was still frustrated from her fight with her dad and still nervous around Poe, but it didn't seem to matter as much. They started walking down the hall, not really going anywhere in particular.

"I didn't know you could paint," Poe said.

He was close enough that his sleeve brushed hers. She wanted to remember every detail because she just knew this kind of luck wouldn't last.

"I just play at it," she said. "Mostly at home. I'm not that good."

He looked at her, lifted an eyebrow. "The butterfly was pretty cool. Better than I can do, that's for sure."

She smiled. "Well, I guess we're even because I really can't sing."

He grinned back. "How bad are you?"

"Really bad. My dad once offered me a raise in my allowance *not* to sing."

Poe laughed and she suddenly didn't feel like the freak

whose mother had *an accident* and whose father was getting weird. She was just a girl walking with a boy.

"I'll keep that in mind," Poe said. "But I'm not as good as I'd like to be either."

"You have a great voice," Beauty argued. "Kinda folky and dark." *Am I flirting? Do I even know how?*

He turned toward her.

"How do you know that?" he asked.

She felt herself flush. She could hardly tell him she sat on her porch and listened to him every Sunday night. He'd think she was stalking him. This was *not* the way to build a relationship. She forced herself to shrug.

"I've heard you. You guys practice near the art room sometimes." She mentally patted herself on the back for a good save.

"I guess I'll have to drop by the art room more often then," he said.

The way he smiled at her made her nervous all over again, but in a good way. It was like he really meant what he was saying.

"I guess you should," she replied, surprising herself.

They both looked up at the bell when it rang.

"Damn," Poe muttered. "Already?" He caught her eye. "What class do you have?"

"Art. You?"

"History."

She nodded as they stood uncertainly, looking at each other. She held up the paintbrush.

"I guess I should wash this before it dries," she said, just to fill the sudden silence.

"I guess so," he said. "I'll see you later."

She nodded again. "Sure."

She wanted to say something more, something clever that would make him laugh or think of her later. But she didn't say anything. She watched him walk away, and before he turned the corner he glanced over his shoulder and winked at her.

— 6 —

BEAUTY SAT AT THE KITCHEN table flipping through a book of Pre-Raphaelite paintings. When the doorbell rang, she frowned. She could barely hear it over the music blaring in the living room. She knew it wasn't her dad. He wouldn't be home until dinner and he would never ring the bell.

She padded softly to the front door and peered through the key hole. Luna's distorted face flashed into view. She was dancing to the music that rattled the windows. She started to sing as Beauty's hand hesitated over the knob.

No one had come to visit since *the accident*, not even Sabrina. She was too nervous about having people see how

she lived, to see their pity or have more rumors flying around at school. She was safer hiding, quiet.

Luna pounded on the door, still dancing. "Hey, B!" she shouted, pounding again.

Beauty sighed. She couldn't very well pretend not to be home. She took a deep breath and opened the door, smiling casually. The scent of roses was strong. Petals were scattered on the porch.

Luna grinned. "Hey, good song."

Beauty nodded, swallowed. "What's up?" she asked.

Luna shrugged. "Not much. Ready to work?"

Beauty frowned. "Work?"

Luna rolled her eyes. "Ten minutes with Poe and you go all gooey on me. Remember? I said I couldn't rehearse with him because we have homework."

Beauty nodded. "I thought you made that up."

"I did, but I figured we should do it anyway. Can I come in or what?"

"Oh." Beauty blinked, stepped aside. "Sure, of course. Sorry."

"I can come back another time if you're busy?"

Beauty bit her lip. This was her opportunity to send Luna home, to keep everything simple and faded. If she sent Luna home, she could go on pretending everything was okay. She shut the door firmly behind Luna.

"No, come on in," she shouted over the music. Beauty led her to the kitchen after turning down the stereo. Luna looked around curiously.

"Cool house," she said. "It's so normal. Unlike mine."

Beauty nearly snorted. "Do you want a drink or something?" she asked. "Juice? Tea?"

"I'd love some tea." Luna dropped down into a wooden chair and opened her knapsack, pulling out books and binders and a pencil case covered in beads and star-shaped sequins.

When the kettle whistled, Beauty poured hot water into the pot to steep the rosehip tea mixture she'd made from her grandmother's recipe. The scent was tart and comforting. Luna spread out her papers and picked up a green felt-tip pen.

"Okay," she said. "We have to figure out what we want to put in this journal and how we should lay it out. Did you get a chance to look through some of the books?"

"A little," Beauty said. "They were basically groupies, right?" she asked hesitantly. "For John Keats' poetry and that critic guy, John Ruskin or whatever?"

Luna grinned. "You're right, actually. I hadn't thought about it that way. We could do something really fun with that." She tapped her pen on her notebook, leaving little marks like stars fallen in the grass. "Why don't we start with our favorite stories or paintings and go from there? You pick the paintings since you're into that."

Beauty poured the tea into cups and then started flipping through the books in front of her as Luna continued to speak. It was nice to have a friend who didn't mind silence, who didn't look at you askance as if trying to figure out if you were going to crack. She recognized Waterhouse's *The Lady of Shalott* and several Rossetti paintings of dark-haired women.

"Okay, my favorite story is about Dante Rossetti," Luna was saying. "He was so creepy, I just love it. He wrote poems for Elizabeth Siddal, who he called 'his Lizzie.' I think she was one of his models as well. Anyway, she was sick a lot and eventually died of an overdose, and Rossetti had all of his poems buried with her."

Beauty glanced up. "That's romantic, not creepy."

Luna leaned back in her chair, looking smug. There was a star rhinestone on her cheek. "That's not all," she said. "A few years later, after several affairs I'm sure, Rossetti decided that he wanted his poems back." Luna paused. "So he had his Lizzie dug up so he could pry the poems from her cold dead hands. He said her hair was still thick and bright, all coiled in a braid."

Beauty blinked. "You made that up."

"Well, maybe the part about her hair, but everything else is true." She sipped at her tea, looking proud of herself.

Beauty shuddered. "That's gross."

"I know. Cool, huh?"

"You are so weird."

"This is true." Luna seemed completely unperturbed by the friendly accusation. "Your turn."

Beauty turned back to the reproductions in front of her. There were several beautiful ones that she liked, and many of them seemed to be attached to some poem or other. "We could show *The Lady of Shalott* and then have the poem next to it," she suggested. "And have Keats' 'Isabella and the Pot of Basil,' which is also creepy by the way, and then show Hunt's painting."

They spent the next hour searching through books for paintings and poems and anecdotes. Beauty thought she might have liked to live in a house full of artists, especially with William Morris and all his hand-painted furniture and medieval fabrics he loved so much. It would be like living in a dream. She could understand now why Luna had claimed to live in a Pre-Raphaelite house.

She couldn't remember the last time she'd hung out at the kitchen table with a friend to do homework. She'd missed this normal feeling. Even the homework was fun, finding out weird details about a bunch of poets and artists who'd lived over a hundred years ago but didn't seem all that different from today's artists. There would always be people who mourned the death of beauty at the hands of technology.

She blinked and rubbed her eyes when the print started to blur a little. She was thinking too hard, trying to absorb too much.

Luna smothered a yawn and smiled sheepishly. "Let's take a break," she suggested, standing up and stretching. "I could use a dance party. Crank up the stereo again."

Beauty ignored the dry scratchy voice of the desert inside and the shy girl who wanted to hide in the attic and decided to just let herself go. It seemed easy when she was with Luna. They listened to song after song, shouted out the lyrics and danced wildly, like dandelions in a strong wind. The roses pressed against the glass. Beauty twirled and twirled until she grew dizzy and collapsed on the couch.

Luna stretched out on the carpet, panting for breath. "Whew," she said. "I needed that."

Beauty lifted handfuls of heavy hair off her sweaty neck and laughed. Luna turned her head, saw the sunlight glinting off glass bottles on a locked cabinet. She frowned curiously.

"How come the liquor cabinet is locked if all of the liquor is out on top? My mother would never trust me like that. No fair."

Beauty's smile faltered. She swallowed. "Dad keeps other stuff in there," she said.

Luna waggled her eyebrows. "Old high school pictures of him with bad hair, or top-secret FBI documents?"

Beauty shook her head, momentarily distracted. "Why is everyone a spy in your world?"

Luna shrugged. "It's more fun that way. So what's in there?" She held up a hand. "You already know I'm rudely nosy, so you don't have to answer."

Beauty took a deep breath, considered what to say. Should she pretend she didn't know? She was pretty sure Luna would then convince her to pick the cabinet's lock. Was this something she was ready to share?

She thought of the way they had turned in circles until the room was a blur of colors and made her decision. "Dad keeps the knives in there," she explained quietly.

Luna turned her head slightly to look at her. "Like hunting gear? Ew."

Beauty shook her head. "Kitchen knives, scissors, needles, anything sharp."

Luna pushed up onto her elbows. "Oh. Why?"

Beauty took a deep breath. "Because of my mother." Luna watched her curiously but didn't say anything. She waited for Beauty to continue. "She didn't just die, she killed herself."

Luna blinked. "Oh, Beauty."

Beauty shrugged, willed her eyes not to water. "Just before summer. She cut her wrists."

Luna got to her feet and sat on the edge of the couch. She looked like she wanted to hug Beauty but wasn't sure if she should. "What's your favorite memory of her?"

Beauty stopped, confused. No one had ever asked her that before. She tilted her head. "I guess being in the garden with her. The way she picked all the roses and put them all over the house." She shrugged. "That sounds dumb."

"No, it doesn't. I don't remember my dad at all. He left before my mom even went into labor."

"Do you hate him?"

"Sometimes."

"What about your mom?"

Luna shrugged. "Star says he was beautiful but they just weren't meant to be together. She says they had one night together and it was special and that's all they needed." She leaned back against the cushions. "That doesn't really help," she admitted. She hesitated. "Why'd your mom do it?"

"She was sick, a chemical imbalance of some kind," Beauty answered, fiddling with the ring on her thumb. "Dad won't really say. But now it's like he's terrified I'm going to do the same thing or something."

"I'm sorry."

Beauty's smile wobbled. "Thanks."

"Is that why you asked me if I'd heard the rumors about you?"

Beauty nodded. "Yeah. It made everyone really uncomfortable for a while. They'd whisper when I came into a room, or everyone would just fall silent and stare at me. I hated it. I still do. Sometimes I wish I was invisible."

Luna squeezed her hand. "Well, if I'm a slut and you're a freak, I guess we're perfect for each other."

Beauty giggled. "I guess so."

— 7 —

I GUESS IT'S WINTER,
*but I don't feel the cold at all, even though I'm wearing a thin
white gown edged with silver ribbons and crystals, and there's
snow everywhere, covering the old garden and the stone wall
that surrounds it. There are hazel bushes and yew under the
snow, and roses everywhere. The roses are in full bloom, white
and perfect and completely untouched by the cold.*

*The cobblestones leading around a marble fountain and toward
a medieval-looking tower are slippery with ice. Everything spar-
kles like the glitter painted on my arms and shoulders. The moon
is fat and high above my head, dressed in a gown of lacy clouds.*

*That's when I notice a long table draped with white velvet
and studded with lit candles, like stars. I see glass jugs filled*

with white wine and apple juice, bowls full of pears and peeled lychee nuts, and cakes sprinkled with icing sugar. There are cups of custard and vanilla ice cream and warm milk.

The table has three place settings, each one marked with a rose: one red, one white and one black. I look around, but I can't see anyone else. The tower is slim and pale, the windows glow with candlelight. On the other side of the wall the forest is thick and shadowy.

I'm mildly surprised when I suddenly see a woman sitting across the table from where I stand in a white throne-like chair. She has pearls around her throat and in her hair, and she's wearing a veil. Her wedding dress is as white as the snow around us.

"Welcome to the feast," she says. Her voice is quiet and soft. Familiar.

When she stands up, her veil blows back and her face is bathed in moonlight.

Rose Dubois. My mother.

I know I'm staring, and I don't care. I don't know what to say. This isn't like the other dreams, not even the one with the cottage. This feels too real, and I want to cry but it's been too long. I'm not sure I remember how.

And in the vast white winter of sorrow I discover a red burning ember of anger.

"Mom?" I say to break the awful silence. I sound annoyed, bratty. I can't help it.

She nods. "It's me, honey."

I've been feeling so little in the last few months and all of a sudden I'm feeling too much at once. I don't know what to do. I sit down heavily in an intricately carved chair.

I realize she's wearing her own wedding dress. I remember it from all the pictures Dad used to have around the house. Now there's just the one, on his dresser, surrounded by vases of roses from the garden.

"Why am I dreaming this?" I ask. "I don't want to be here. I want to wake up."

"Not yet, Beauty. Not yet."

I cross my arms and scowl. "What happened, Mom?" I whisper. It's the one thing I never got to ask her. "Why? Was it something we did? Or didn't do?"

"I fell asleep, Beauty," she tells me sadly. "It seemed like the easiest thing to do."

"You left us."

She nods. Her eyes are watery and a tear falls down her cheek. It makes me mad. She can cry and I still can't. And even though I'm furious and hurt and confused, I still miss her.

"I'm sorry, Beauty. I didn't know what else to do."

"Was it me?" I think about the dream I had, the one where she's lying in a bathtub of roses. I didn't know then that it was a premonition. I didn't know.

"It was me," she answers. "Just me. You aren't to blame."

"I don't believe you."

She tries to smile. "Stay. Eat with me."

I shake my head. Ice cream isn't going to make everything better. At this point I don't know if anything can. My mother left me and then I left myself.

"I have to get out of here," I say.

"Beauty, I love you."

I don't look at her. Instead I stare at the glass plate in front of me, a white rose in its center. I'm not mad anymore. I feel deflated, sad. I wonder for the hundredth time if I could have stopped her. If I'd told her about my dream, would things have been different?

I can see my reflection in the plate. My face is as pale as the moon over me and the white dress billowing around my ankles. I hate it. I don't want to look at myself for a second longer.

I pick up the plate and hurl it to the ground where it shatters, glittering in the snow like ice. My mother sighs, reaches out a hand toward me.

"Oh, Beauty," she says. "Be careful."

I turn away from her and start to run down the path. I don't know where I'm going. The shattered fragments of the plate have cut into my feet and blood seeps into the snow. I barely notice. My mother's screams follow me.

"Beauty, there will be another dream. The third one is always the most dangerous."

I shake my head and keep running.

"Remember your name," she says, but her voice is fading. "You're beautiful, don't ever forget that."

When I wake up I'm outside in the garden, standing in the middle of the white roses and shivering in the cold night air.

$$— 8 —$$

BEAUTY KNOCKED ON LUNA'S
front door and waited, feeling as if she was about to step into
an adventure. It always felt like that in Luna's house. Every
corner held some impossible curiosity or a muse waiting
for you to join her for tea. The wind picked up in the street
behind her and Beauty shivered. Autumn was developing
teeth early this year.

The door creaked open and Luna's mother poked her
head out. The sunlight caught the purple in her hair and the
silver hoop in her right nostril.

"You must be Beauty," she said, motioning her inside. She
hugged Beauty, enveloping her in cinnamon and vanilla and

the lingering traces of incense. "Luna's told me all about you. I'm Star."

Beauty smiled, wondering how she should act. Her regular parents-of-friends manner seemed too stiff for Star. She certainly didn't look like a typical mother. She was wearing a paint-splattered kimono and a multitude of silver bangles.

"It's nice to meet you, Ms. Bird," Beauty said. "Thanks for letting me stay over tonight."

Star waved her hand, laughing. "Honey, call me Star or I'll feel positively ancient." She closed the door. "Luna's in her room. Can you find it?"

Beauty nodded shyly. "I think so."

"Good, go on up. And don't mind Trumayne if you see him. He's in one of his infamous moods." She winked. "It just means he'll do some brilliant work tonight. I hear you're an artist too."

Beauty felt herself blushing. "Not really. I'm just learning."

"Nonsense," Star scoffed. "An artist is born, not made, and I can see you've got the spirit of an artist. You just let her out and shame the devil." She rolled her eyes. "I'm in lecture mode. You'd better escape while you still can."

Beauty went up the stairs, dragging her sleeping bag and her knapsack. She felt a little like she'd just been swept down a tumbling river. She could definitely see where Luna got it from. She smiled to herself as she headed down the hallway toward the second set of stairs. The carpet was wearing thin in spots, and she heard a crash and a curse when she passed a closed door painted an eye-scorching shade of magenta.

Farther along, she glimpsed Simone through a half-open door. Her long blond hair settled around her shoulders, and her feet were bare again. She looked like she belonged in one of the Pre-Raphaelite paintings Beauty was falling in love with. She decided she would use Simone as a model for Keats' "La Belle Dame Sans Merci" or maybe for Shakespeare's Titania, Queen of the Faeries. The thought made her smile. Maybe Star was right; there was an artist inside her who just needed to be set free.

She took a deep breath. Even the air tasted different here. She could almost feel all of her worries and doubts fading away like a tapestry left too long in the sun. This was the one place where she could truly feel like an artist, like someone with a voice.

She knocked softly on Luna's door. It whipped open and Luna blinked at her.

"Hi!" Luna said. "About time you got here!"

Beauty blinked back. "What's up?"

"Should I call Kennedy?" Luna twisted her hands together. Her collarbones were dusted with glitter.

Beauty dropped her stuff and tilted her head. "You're acting like a girl," she said, a little awestruck.

Luna frowned. "I am a girl." She plucked at her T-shirt. "Mind you, I think my boobs got lost in the mail."

Beauty made a sound that was half-snort, half-laugh. "I know the feeling. I just meant, you never seem to get worked up over guys and stuff. And you're not exactly shy."

Luna sighed and flopped onto the beanbag chair. Incense burned on the windowsill next to thick white candles. "I know." She pushed to her feet again and started to pace. "I don't know, it's different with Kennedy. I get all nervous." She winced. "I'm afraid he'll laugh at me," she admitted.

Beauty rolled her eyes. "Welcome to my world," she said dryly. "Kennedy will love you. You're totally his type."

Luna stopped, grinned wickedly. "I am, aren't I?" She twirled once, hands outstretched. Her glance was full of mischief. "You're Poe's type too, you know."

Beauty shook her head. "I'm not anyone's type," she replied wistfully. "I'm not even sure I *am* a type. I look in the mirror and I don't see anything. I'm boring."

Luna crossed her arms. "You are not," she declared. "I don't hang out with boring people."

"You do now. I mean, look at me. Boring hair, boring clothes, boring little nothing."

Luna shook her head. "Don't talk about yourself that way. Besides, you can look any way you want to. I'll help."

"I don't have your kind of courage." But a small flower poked its nervous head above ground. Beauty's fingers began to tingle. "I don't think."

"Ha!" Luna pounced on her, grabbed her hands. "Come on, let's go."

Beauty dug in her heels. "Where?"

Luna pulled on her hand. "We're going to have a make-over. We'll work from the outside in. I'll even teach you how to scream."

Her enthusiasm was contagious. Beauty laughed. "My dad'll kill me."

She let herself be dragged downstairs, through Star's bedroom, which was surprisingly sparse, and into the adjoining bathroom. Jewelry boxes lined the shelves, stuffed to overflowing. Perfumes and candles and scented body soaps were jumbled into baskets along the side of the white claw-foot bathtub. Luna pulled another basket out from under the sink. It held more hair dyes than the average drugstore.

Beauty watched Luna carefully. "What did you have in mind?"

Luna held up a large tube of dye triumphantly. "We're going to make your hair the same color as those roses you love so much."

Beauty's eyes widened. "We are?"

"Definitely."

"That's awfully red."

"That's the point."

Beauty swallowed. "I don't know if I can pull that off."

Luna rolled her eyes. "Of course you can. Don't think so much."

Beauty looked at her reflection. Her long hair was simple and brown, the same as it had been for years now. She looked at herself and didn't feel anything, didn't see anything that made her real. She wanted the beauty of Guinevere, the glitter of Ophelia, the danger of Nimue. But she wouldn't get any of that by hiding.

"Okay," she found herself saying. "Let's do it."

Luna all but squealed with excitement. "This is going to be so cool," she said. "Come on, let's get you set up."

"Won't your mom mind?"

Luna shook her head. "No, in fact, I'll go get her. She can help us out. She's great with hair stuff."

It was decidedly surreal to be sitting on the floor of her friend's mom's bathroom, drinking cinnamon coffee, while said friend's mom worked dye through her hair.

"This will be a great color on you," Star said, stripping off her rubber gloves and tossing them in the sink. There was a tattoo on the inside of her elbow. Beauty wondered briefly if Luna had ever brought her mom to kindergarten for show-and-tell.

"This needs to set for a bit so I'll let you and Luna chat. Help yourself to anything in the studio for your project," she said. "But don't touch the oil paints." She wiggled her eyebrows. "And don't pierce anything," she ordered.

Beauty shook her head, careful not to splatter. "This is so weird," she said. "But thanks. And thanks for letting me sleep over. Dad was freaking out about having to work so late tonight."

Luna leaned back against the cupboards and stretched her legs out in front of her.

"It's totally cool. Besides, we still have to finish up the journal for class tomorrow so it's perfect." She crossed her ankles. "We should make our own artistic society, like the PRB did."

Beauty thought about having hair like rose petals and painting all day. "Yeah," she said, surprising herself again. "We should."

They decided on the layout for their journal, spreading out all their notes on the cold tiles. They punched holes into the pages and bound them together with blue ribbons. They decided it gave the journal a more old-fashioned, cozy feel.

The egg timer by the sink rang. It was time to rinse out Beauty's hair. She knelt on a folded towel and hung her head into the tub. White porcelain filled her vision. Luna extended the showerhead and fiddled with the taps until the water was warm. It was awkward, but she managed to hang over the side enough to aim the water through all of Beauty's long hair.

The water hit the tub with a soft rhythm, the sound of rain on a small lake. It was vaguely hypnotic, but the water was bright as roses and looked too much like blood swirling down the drain. Beauty thought of her recent dreams and of the one that had haunted her since *the accident*: her mother lying in a white tub filled with red red flowers. Blood would have filled the bath and tainted the water. She would have watched it, waited for it.

Beauty gagged, tears burning her eyes. She didn't hear Luna calling her name until she touched her arm. Beauty jerked and scrambled back, her hair whipping out and spraying the bathroom with water. She didn't realize she was crying until she stopped to wonder why her tongue tasted salty.

And then she kept crying, tears falling down her cheeks and running down her neck. She remained on her knees, letting everything around her blur. She was vaguely aware of Luna kissing her cheek and then rubbing her back and calling for Star.

She was a river, a lake, a waterfall.

WHEN BEAUTY WOKE UP it took her several moments to figure out where she was. The bed was unfamiliar and the pictures lining the wall beside her were of tragic-looking women in pale gowns. The room smelled like sandalwood and vanilla perfume. The lights were off and it was getting dark outside. Candles in bowls burned on the desk.

She'd slept without dreaming and felt strangely lighter, calmer. Her throat ached a little and her eyes were sore, but she felt better than she had in a long time. She rubbed her lids and sat up, stretching her back. Her hair fell over her arms.

Hearing movement, Luna looked up from where she was adding some finishing touches to their project. Her smile was subdued. "Feel better?" she asked.

Beauty brought her knees up to her chest, remembering. "I'm a little embarrassed," she said. "I'm sorry I lost it like that."

"It's okay." Luna handed her a cup of warm tea. "It's chamomile. Star swears it's the most soothing tea on earth."

Beauty cradled the mug in her hands and tried to smile. It was surprisingly simple. "Thanks. I hope I didn't scare you."

Luna grinned with her characteristic zeal. "Are you kidding? Clare with PMS would scare me. This was nothing."

Beauty chuckled and sipped the tea before setting it down and stretching. "What time is it?"

"Just past seven. I'm almost done the rest of the journal."
Beauty looked guilty. "I'm sorry for that too."

Luna shrugged one shoulder negligently. "There wasn't much left to do." She bit her lip. "I guess dyeing your hair wasn't such a good idea," she said. "I'm sorry if I bullied you into it."

Beauty stroked her hair, smiling. "I love it," she assured her friend. "It's perfect."

"Star says you just needed to open the door."

"I think she's right," Beauty murmured. She *did* feel like the air could move through her, like she was an attic recently cleaned of cobwebs and trunks filled with old dresses that didn't fit anymore. It was a wonderful feeling.

She looked at the paintings on the walls with a crooked smile. She pointed to *The Sleeping Princess* by Edward Burne-Jones.

"That," Beauty said. "That's who I want to look like."

Luna followed her finger and stood slowly. "Are you sure you're up for it? You don't want to lie down some more?"

"I think I'm tired of lying down."

Luna seemed to sense the switch in her mood and clapped her hands, creating a distraction.

"Great. I know just the thing." She disappeared into the chaos of her closet for a few minutes while Beauty turned on the stereo. Delerium's *Karma* flooded the room. Beauty thought she could step right into a Pre-Raphaelite painting.

Luna was throwing clothes behind her onto the floor and muttering to herself.

"Should I be scared?" Beauty joked.

Luna emerged with a butterfly clip hanging over her eye, shaking off a tangle of clothes that had fallen off the rack and onto her head. She surveyed everything with a critical eye, like a prospector. Anticipation was nectar on Beauty's tongue.

Luna tossed her a simple white eyelet shirt with cap sleeves and a pair of hip-hugger cords the same color as Beauty's hair, hemmed with ribbons and beads. There were quilt-like patches on the bottom. She added a skirt with a matching ribbon along the bottom.

"Put those on," she said, marching over to her jewelry boxes. "We'll start simple and very you." She winked and started to pick through beads and crystals and Victorian-style monstrosities. Once Beauty had slipped into the clothes, she waited, fiddling with the ring on her thumb.

Luna looked over. "Put on the skirt too."

Beauty blinked. "Over the jeans?"

Luna laughed. "I promise it'll look good. Just trust me."

Beauty wiggled into the skirt and started to turn around to look at herself in the mirror hanging inside the closet door.

"Ah!" Luna stopped her. "Don't you dare. We're not done yet. You wanted a look, we're going to give you a look."

Beauty shifted her weight from foot to foot. "You're bossy," she said amiably.

Luna nodded. "I am. All divas are." She batted her eyelashes. "And soon you will be one of us."

Beauty recoiled in mock terror. Luna ignored her and snapped a necklace around her neck. She added thick silver bracelets and an anklet. She brushed out Beauty's hair and tugged and fussed and braided until Beauty was squirming with impatience.

"Are you done yet?" Beauty asked.

Luna mumbled something vaguely rude through the clips clamped between her lips. She finally stepped back, folded her arms over her chest and took a good look. She nodded slowly. "Okay," she decided. "You can look now."

Beauty turned slowly toward the mirror. She'd hated her reflection for months now and part of her was nervous and scared of what she might see. Even in borrowed clothes she was just Beauty Dubois, quiet and lonely.

But even she had to admit that the mixture of fabrics and styles made her look like a Pre-Raphaelite bohemian who time-traveled in her spare time. Glitter sparkled on her arms and cheeks. Her hair fell down her arms with a simple braid at each temple, tied off with an elastic and decorated with rhinestone-covered rose barrettes. Silver gleamed at her wrists and she wore an elaborate crystal Victorian-style choker suited to a faery queen or a slightly wild artist. Her feet were bare.

Luna chewed on her lower lip. "Well?" she demanded anxiously. She barely paused. "You hate it. I knew it. It's too much. You should lie down again."

Beauty chuckled. She wasn't tired anymore, wasn't drained or afraid. The girl in the mirror was borrowed, but she was a step in the right direction. Her smile widened. "I love it," she said.

— 9 —

BEAUTY FLIPPED THROUGH the journal Luna had finished putting together. Paintings and poems crowded each other. She ran a finger over *The Lady of Shalott.*

"Anything else you need me to do? I feel really bad that you had to finish this on your own."

"It was fun. You could draw something for the cover though. It's too bland like that," said Luna.

Beauty glanced at the title, written plainly on the cream-colored paper. It certainly didn't fit the riot of colors and words inside. She quelled the instinctive thought that she wasn't talented enough to draw the cover. It didn't matter if she was or she wasn't. She was going to do it.

"Okay," Beauty said. "Do you have any pencils?"

Luna snorted. "Are you kidding? My mother has cupboards full of pencils and pastels and all that stuff. And she's got drawing paper too. We could rip the edges of your drawing and then glue it on the cover so it looks old."

"Cool. On one condition though."

Luna glanced up at her. "What's that?"

Beauty picked up Luna's phone, which was covered in sequined cloth, and handed it to her.

"Call Kennedy."

Luna shrank away. "What?"

Beauty had to grin. "My turn to be the bully," she said. "I'll draw and stand up in front of the class for this project if you call Kennedy right now."

Luna swallowed. "Geez, get a load of you," she joked. "A new outfit and suddenly you're the queen of the castle."

Beauty looked briefly proud of herself. "That's right."

Luna groaned. "I created a monster. All right," she continued in a rush. "Give me the phone before I lose my nerve." She wiped suddenly damp palms on her jeans. "Mom's studio is downstairs, turn left. It's the purple door covered with stars. Help yourself to whatever you need," she added, not looking away from the phone. She thought it might be laughing at her.

Beauty smiled to herself and closed the door behind her. Luna had already helped her more than she would ever know. She could at least try and return the favor. She went down the stairs and peered at the doors until she found the one she was looking for. The windows were dark, the gardens swallowed by night. More candles burned in bowls all over the empty studio. Beauty was beginning to think Star either couldn't afford electricity or that her best friend made candles for a living. Either way it made the comfortably shabby house even more beautiful.

Beauty stood at the drawing table and ran her fingers over its scarred surface. She wanted a table like this so badly she could taste it. It felt good to want something that badly. Maybe she'd ask her father to build her one.

She found a pad of thick drawing paper, loving the feel of the heavy stock. Tins of pencils and brushes lined the back of the table, in front of the wide window. There was a half-empty box of Conté-crayons by her elbow. She was sure the armoire behind her was full of pastels and watercolor pencils and perfectly sharpened charcoal pencils, but she felt weird going through Star's stuff when she wasn't here.

She didn't resist the urge to stand there in the thin shadows and sketch on the paper, first thinking of the journal and then of nothing except the pleasure of Conté scratching against white paper.

Her eye was caught by a postcard of a painting of a woman lying back in a river choked by bushes and weeds. Her hands were pale as lilies and opened to the sky. Her mouth was partially open as if she had drowned reciting a favorite poem. Her white lace dress was covered with poppies and violets, and her hair was the same color as the brown water. Beauty glanced at the back. "J.E. Millais *Ophelia.*" She thought of the painting she'd been struggling with for weeks, the one of her mother. The one she'd torn apart in a fit of temper.

This was what she'd been trying to capture, this tragic beauty, this pause between before and after. *The accident* somehow made mythic, made to be a story she might understand. *Ophelia, La Jeune Martyre, The Lady of Shalott.*

This was how she would paint her mother—asleep in her white wedding dress and crowned with roses. It might make sense then.

She turned to a fresh page and began to sketch her ideas, surrounded by the warm glow of candlelight. She went through several sheets and it almost felt as if her hands were birds, skimming and darting of their own accord. The images were rough, but they were a good start. She smiled at them before gathering them up and leaving to get some gossip out of Luna.

She nearly screamed when she saw the shadow standing in the doorway, watching her. She recalled the woman in black who watched her, watched her in her sleep. Her heart stuttered briefly before the figure spoke.

"Beauty?"

She nodded and her heart began a whole new dance. She would know that voice anywhere. Poe smiled at her. His hair was pulled back. He was wearing dark jeans, a black T-shirt and holding his guitar case.

"I didn't mean to scare you," he said.

"That's okay," Beauty said. "I didn't hear you, that's all." She wondered how long he'd been standing there.

"You look great," he added, taking in her clothes and her braids. "Cool hair."

She wondered if jumping up and down and whooping for joy might be a bit much. She settled for a wider smile.

"Thanks," she replied with what she hoped was a relatively steady voice. "Luna's handiwork."

He shrugged. "You were pretty before too."

She really really wanted to kiss him. They looked at each other for a long moment, all silence and candlelight. She loved the way the shadows caught his cheekbones and his dark eyes. His earphones were around his neck as usual. She thought of the dream she'd had of his mouth on hers and struggled not to blush.

"So, what are you doing here?" they both said at the same time and then laughed self-consciously.

Poe put down his guitar case and stepped farther into the room. He leaned against the wall.

"I'm sleeping over," Beauty explained. "You?"

"I was practicing a new song. I come and play with Eric sometimes. Ever met him?"

Beauty shook her head. "How many people live here anyway?"

Poe rolled his eyes. "Tons. And they keep changing. It's worse than living with all of my brothers."

She felt suddenly shy and glanced at the room. She wondered if he was just being polite. Maybe she should excuse herself before things got really awkward. She would just die if he got bored and left.

"Are you busy right now?" Poe asked. "Was I interrupting?"

She smiled. He didn't want to get away from her as quickly as possible after all. "No, I'm done. I was just sketching something for our project tomorrow."

"Can I see?"

She nibbled on her lower lip. "Um, I guess so." She handed the sketches over to him with a nervous laugh. "They're really rough."

He bent his head and looked at them, shuffling through each page. When he looked up he was very serious. "You lied to me," he said.

She blinked. "What?" She was half-confused, half-insulted. "When?" she demanded.

The corner of his mouth curved slightly. "You said you weren't a very good artist," he explained. "But you are."

Air rushed out of her tense lungs. "That's an interesting way to pay me a compliment," she grumbled.

He laughed. "Sorry. Listen, if you're not busy or anything, do you want to hang out for a bit?"

"Right now?"

"Yeah. Unless you can't?"

She could see him struggling not to show disappointment. She wondered whose fairy-tale life she'd fallen into. Whatever the case, she wasn't giving it back any time soon.

"No, I've got some time."

He grinned. "Great."

Poe slid down along the wall and sat with his legs crossed. Beauty sat too. The hardwood floors of the studio gleamed with flickering firelight. Part of her wanted to stay here forever and another part wanted to rush upstairs to tell Luna what was happening.

They looked at each other. As the pause lengthened, Beauty grew flustered. She tried to think of a question to ask to get him talking. She wasn't going to be that shy girl who didn't have anything to say and didn't care. She blurted out the first thing that came to mind and hoped it wasn't totally lame. "I didn't know you had a tattoo."

He glanced down at the black design that poked out from under his left sleeve. "Yeah, my brother took me before school started. Mom was not pleased."

"Can I see it?" She tilted her head and wanted to cheer herself for her boldness. She wanted to ask Luna if all of her clothes were magic or if it was maybe just the hair dye. Poe lifted up his sleeve and showed the tribal armband on his sleekly muscled arm. Beauty wasn't quite ready to reach over and touch it, but she really wanted to.

"Cool," she said instead. "Did it hurt?"

"Hurt like hell," he admitted. "I know it's not macho for me to admit this, but it was the sound of the needle that really creeped me out. It was worse than being at the dentist."

She smiled. "Well, it looks good." Her words seemed to hang in the air. She blushed and tried to find something else to say to cover up the echo. Poe let his sleeve drop and looked at her.

"I like your ring," he said, taking her hand and brushing his thumb over it. His palm was warm against hers. Her stomach did a somersault but in a good way.

"Do you know we've been going to the same school practically since birth and I don't really know you?" he asked, still holding her hand as if it was the most natural thing in the world.

"Not much to know, really," she said. "You've heard the rumors."

He looked her right in the eye and nodded. She liked that he didn't squirm or pretend not to know what she meant.

"People talk too much," he said.

"I'd have to agree."

"Want to talk about it?"

"Not really," she said honestly. Something had bloomed today, some little bit of healing, but she wasn't ready to explain it. She was glad Luna knew and it was enough for now.

He nodded. "Okay. Do you have a boyfriend?"

"No." She didn't want to ask if he had a girlfriend, afraid to ruin the moment, but she did. "You?"

He shook his head. "No boyfriend."

She rolled her eyes. "I meant girlfriend."

"Oh." His eyes twinkled. "Nope. What's your favorite movie?"

She blinked at the rapid change of topic. "I don't know, *The Last of the Mohicans*, maybe."

"Mine's *The Thing*. Okay, your turn."

She raised her eyebrows. "My turn for what?"

"Your turn in the question game. Ask me something."

She tapped the fingers of her free hand on the floor as she considered. She settled for something easy to start with. "Favorite band?"

He nodded. "Good choice, good choice. I'd have to say The Tea Party and Radiohead. You?"

"The Grapes of Wrath."

"Favorite writer?"

"Jane Austen."

He lifted one eyebrow. "I'll have to remember that."

"What about you?"

"Not Edgar Allan Poe, much to everyone's surprise."

She chuckled. "I'll remember that too."

"Favorite song?"

She thought about all of the nights she'd spent on her porch listening to him practice old songs. "The Doors, 'Waiting for the Sun.'"

He leaned closer to her.

"One last question," he said.

"Okay." She tried not to show her disappointment. She could easily sit here all night with him. "What?"

"Can I kiss you?"

She just stared at him for a moment. She resisted the urge to shake her head to make sure she'd heard right. Her stomach dipped into a full-fledged ballet routine complete with costumes.

"Beauty?" he asked nervously. Her eyes snapped back to his. He was close enough that his breath was warm on her cheek. His mouth was inches from hers as he waited for her to answer. Dream images flashed before her eyes, the way he held his head, the flickering of the candles. It was exactly as she'd dreamt. Even down to the feel of the hardwood floor under her and his hand on her knee.

She closed the distance between them and brushed her mouth against his. She felt him smile against her lips and his hand ran up her arm and tangled into her hair at the nape of her neck. He smelled like soap and leaves, like a jungle.

She was a candle, a torch, a flame.

BEAUTY MET LUNA'S EYES
in the mirror of the school washroom on the second floor.

"I don't know about this," Beauty said. "Ever heard of
baby steps?"

Luna applied another coat of glitter lip gloss and shook
her head. "I firmly believe in jumping into the deep end.
You learn to swim faster."

Beauty snorted. "Or you drown."

Sabrina, perched on the counter, swinging her feet,
laughed. "You look great," she said. "Weird, but great."

Beauty rolled her eyes. "Gee, thanks."

Sabrina rolled her eyes right back, grinning.

Beauty smoothed her hands over the dress she'd been
convinced, or bullied rather, to wear. It was pale with long

layers and cinched tightly at the waist. She wore several long strands of jet beads, and her red hair was wrapped into a messy bun. Luna stood next to her, in a similar dress of pale yellow. She wore a cameo at her throat and a large hat.

"We are going to be laughed at," Beauty groaned. "I don't know why I let you talk me into this."

"Are you kidding?" Luna winked. "After you and Poe last night, I could do no wrong."

Beauty blushed slightly.

Sabrina shook her head at Luna. "What have you done to our quiet little Beauty?"

They grinned at each other until Beauty poked them both in the arm. "Could we focus on my panicking, please? I still don't know about this," she swallowed audibly. "Poe's in that class. What if he laughs at me?"

Luna rolled her eyes. "He would never. Besides, he's gaga over you."

"Gaga?"

She nodded firmly. "That's what I said. Gaga. It's a technical term."

Beauty laughed and Luna linked her arm through hers. "Now come on, let's go conquer English class. Kingsley will be wowed to his toes and give us As on the spot."

Luna didn't seem to notice the other students staring at them as they hurried down the hall to class. Beauty tried not to squirm. Regardless of what had happened, being gawked at was still not one of her favorite things. She nearly hid behind a door when they passed Clare.

Clare snickered. "Nice outfits."

Luna rushed right past her without a single glance. Clare stared after them, slightly put off.

"That girl is way too high-maintenance," Luna muttered as they ducked into the classroom. "She needs to do yoga or something."

"Here goes nothing," Beauty muttered back as the class fell silent, looking at them with widening eyes. Somebody whistled. Mr. Kingsley glanced up.

"Girls," he said with a questioning smile. "I guess you're ready for your presentation."

Luna curtsied. Beauty just swallowed.

"This is Elizabeth Eleanor Siddal," Luna introduced Beauty with a flourish before handing out copies of their journal entitled "The Seed." When Beauty spoke, she tried not to rush her words.

"I was an artist's model for several of the Pre-Raphaelite Brotherhood, such as John Millais, Willian Holman-Hunt and Dante Rossetti, who encouraged my painting and later became my husband."

Someone giggled. Sabrina aimed a glare at them. The class stared at Beauty and Luna, awed, nervous and interested despite themselves. Beauty wiped her palms on her borrowed dress. She refused to look at Poe.

"I was very ill, but I had an exhibition of my work in 1857. I painted *Lady Clare* and *Lady Affixing A Pennant To A Knight's Spear*. I also helped with the decoration of William Morris's Red House. I loved to paint, but history would rather remember me as a silent artist's model and a muse who died young. You won't find me in a traditional textbook."

She stepped back, blushing, when she was done. Luna threw a grin over her shoulder and then turned to face the class. "I am Christina Rossetti," she said.

Unlike Beauty, Luna sounded confident, her pace slow and unhurried. Only Beauty saw the slight tremble in her fingers. It made her feel better somehow, less alone. "I was born in 1830 into a very artistic family," continued Luna. "I have two brothers, William and Dante Rossetti. Poetry is my art and I wrote several verses for the PRB journal *The Germ*. I also wrote 'The Goblin Market.'"

As Luna read passages from "The Goblin Market," Beauty picked up a piece of chalk and began to sketch on the blackboard. She brought the poem to life, drawing simple images of pomegranates, a goblin man with a basket, and two women holding hands. She could feel Poe's eyes on her back, and when she glanced over her shoulder, he grinned at her. It was the first she'd seen of him since their kiss in Star's studio. She wondered if he'd told his friends.

Luna continued to read from John Keats' "La Belle Dame Sans Merci" and Tennyson's "The Lady of Shalott."

When they were finished, they curtsied briefly again. Mr. Kingsley nodded, unfolding himself from his chair.

"Very interesting, girls. Very original."

Luna gave Beauty a knowing look. The bell rang. The classroom erupted into a cacophony of noise as twenty-odd students rushed the door at the same time. The hallway was already shaking with the pounding of footsteps. Luna drew Beauty into a corner and squealed. "We were amazing!" She poked Beauty. "Admit it, you loved it."

Beauty tilted her head, tried not to grin. "We did okay."

Luna rolled her eyes. "Give me a break."

"Okay, okay, we were wonderful, divine. They will talk about us in these halls long after we're dead."

"Much better," Luna approved.

"But this dress is really uncomfortable."

Luna laughed. "I know."

"Hey, Luna," Paul sneered as he passed them. "You guys were really lame."

Beauty's face fell. She refused to turn around and let him see it. Luna glared at him over Beauty's shoulder.

"Go away," she said simply. She lowered her voice and whispered to Beauty. "I went out with him too. Apparently he thought he was going to get lucky."

Beauty sighed. "He's famous for it. Or thinks he is, anyway."

Paul kept sneering. "Why don't you and your freak mother go back to where you came from?"

Beauty tossed her hair over her shoulder and turned around very slowly. "Now who's lame?" she asked lightly. She was not smiling. She was tired to death of the Clares and the Pauls of Briar High. She'd let them intimidate her for too long. Paul just stared at her. "Just because Luna has taste and you didn't get any is no reason to be a jerk. Get a grip on yourself," said Beauty. One of Paul's friends laughed. Paul's nostrils flared. Beauty just stared him down and then waved her hands. "Shoo."

Luna waited until they were out of earshot before she burst into laughter. Sabrina emerged from the classroom behind them, clapping loudly. Beauty curtsied.

BEAUTY WAS SMILING when she pushed open the front door. The roses crowded her on either side, blooms fading. Petals sprinkled the ground like rain. She'd only been gone for a day, but it felt like a year. She half-expected the house to look different. It didn't.

She poured herself a glass of juice and sighed over the perfectly cubed cheese and sliced watermelon. Something had to be done. They couldn't keep living like this. She ignored the plate her father had prepared for her and grabbed a handful of chocolate chip cookies instead.

Chewing contentedly, she turned on her computer and decided to check her e-mails without even bothering to remove her coat. Sabrina had sent her a couple of messages. There was a chain letter forward, which she deleted immediately, and an advertisement promising to cure her male pattern baldness.

Her hands froze over the keyboard when she saw Poe's name. The subject of his e-mail had been left blank.

She smiled and jiggled her foot nervously. She opened the message and read it quickly. She felt self-conscious suddenly, as if he was watching her.

Hey Beauty, Just wanted to say hi. Great presentation today in class. You look cute in long dresses. I stopped by your locker after school, but I guess I just missed you. Had a great time yesterday. Want to do something maybe this weekend? Poe.

Beauty had never squealed before in her entire life. She made up for it now. She also jumped to her feet and did a dance of joy, which mostly consisted of flailing herself about until she got tired. She plopped back down into her chair, still grinning and panting.

She decided Luna had to see the e-mail directly, and she'd call Sabrina tonight and tell her everything. She hit forward and typed in a quick message, barely glancing at the screen as she tried to figure out what she would write in her e-mail to Poe. It would have to be casual and witty and, of course, perfect.

Luna, you are queen of the world. You have magic clothes. Can you believe it? Does he even know how beautiful he is? This is so unbelievably cool, I think I might throw up. Beauty.

She hit the send button and sat back in her chair. She wanted to sound casual but interested and definitely not like all the other girls who probably e-mailed Poe. She bit her lower lip and stared at the screen thoughtfully, focusing.

Something in the bottom of her belly turned over slowly and then began to spin around like pollen caught in a high wind. She grew very still except for the rapid blinking of her eyes as she focused.

"No," she whispered. She touched the screen. "No, no, no." Her e-mail service was telling her, clear as day, that she had not hit "forward" but "reply." Her e-mail wasn't whirling through cyberspace on its way to Luna's mailbox. It was being shot straight toward Poe. "No!" she yelled and slapped the back button as many times as she could. She couldn't cancel the e-mail or retrieve it or change it.

She couldn't even crawl into a hole and die.

She jumped to her feet and began to pace back and forth, back and forth. Her hands flapped as she talked to herself.

"It's okay," she told herself in a falsely calm voice. "I'll just leave town. People do it all the time. I'll get a new identity. They've got to have some kind of witness protection program for idiots." She groaned. "I hate computers." She turned to glare at the offensive machine in question and then picked up the phone and dialed Luna's number. "I really really hate computers," she said without preamble.

"What?" Luna asked. "Beauty?"

"I'm running away. Wanna come with me?"

"What happened?"

Beauty paced again even though the phone cord only stretched about two feet.

"I just sent you an e-mail," she said.

"Okay. Should I turn on my computer?"

"Don't bother. I forwarded a message Poe sent me with a note. Only, instead of hitting forward, I hit reply." There was a pause on the other end of the line. Beauty nodded sharply. "Exactly."

Luna sucked in her breath. "Forwarding is a dangerous dangerous thing."

Beauty laughed. The sound was too loud and slightly ragged at the edges.

"I'm never going to school again. This is probably the most mortifyingly embarrassing thing that has ever happened to me. Worse than the egg salad incident in grade three."

"What egg salad incident?" Luna was trying not to giggle.

"Never mind." Beauty dropped back into the chair. "Oh, Luna, what am I going to do?"

"Laugh at yourself and assume Poe has a sense of humor?"

Beauty snorted. "That's no fun at all. Next."

"That's all I've got."

"There's got to be something else I can do. Things were going so well. This is so unfair."

Luna sighed. "I know, but I really think it will be all right."

"I'm going to go sulk."

"Try not to hurt yourself." She could hear Luna grinning into the phone. As she hung up, she heard her dad open the door and call out for her. She sighed. She really wanted to pout, but now she had to go and talk to her dad first. Then she'd consider setting her computer on fire.

Her father smiled and hugged her. "Hi, honey, did you have fun last night?"

Beauty nodded and hugged him back. "Yeah, it was great. And I think Mr. Kingsley really liked our presentation."

"I'm sure he did." Her father frowned when she stepped back and sunlight poured through the windows like honey, catching sticky fingers over the brooch on her jacket. He grabbed her shoulder.

"What's that?" he asked.

She blinked. "Oh, I dyed my hair."

"Not that." He sounded tense.

She frowned. "What?" His angry gaze burned at the brooch on the pocket of her jacket. She closed her eyes briefly. The sun glinted off the tarnished metal. "Oh."

"You know the rules, Beauty."

Her jaw clenched. It took a moment for her to realize she was mad, not scared or worried or invisible. Just mad. It felt good. She could still feel the weird dream around her, like a red veil over her skin. She thought of the little girl and her warnings and of her mother. Everything had changed in the last few days, and yet everything was still the same.

She shook her head and yanked at the pin, nearly ripping the denim.

"This is a brooch, Dad," she explained snidely. She knew it was a tone that had "grounded" written all over it. "Girls wear them. It's jewelry."

"Be careful with that."

She rolled her eyes. "It's not a machete, it's a brooch." She flipped the pin out and jabbed it into her finger. Blood welled on the tip like a ruby. "See?" she shouted. "I pricked my finger and I'm still alive."

Her dad paled until he was roughly the color of milk. She had a flash of guilt and worry that he might pass out. He looked like he was made of paper. He shook his head and she could see that he was trembling when he walked away, letting the back door slam behind him.

She watched him go and sucked on her finger and thought her blood tasted the same as it had in that first dream.

SHE STOMPED UPSTAIRS, wanting to cry. Everything had been going so well and now it was right back the way it had always been. She was alone and stupid to think she could have changed herself, could have grown stronger and freer. Luna had unleashed something inside her, and Poe had kissed her and brought bloom to a dead garden, but was it really worth it when everything just hurt so much? She had been better off when she couldn't cry and couldn't feel anything.

Surely being numb was better than this? She crawled under her covers and pulled them over her head. She drifted off to sleep and, below her, her garden grew. Roses pushed their way out of the stems, elongating and gathering over the front door in dozens of colors: red, white, peach, pink, yellow.

The doorknob disappeared beneath a tangle of thorns.

I GUESS MY MOM WAS RIGHT.

There's always a third dream.

I'm standing on the edge of that forest, between the dark trees and the warm glow of candles from the courtyard garden where I sat with my mother. It's midnight and the moon is as full and white as a wedding veil above me. The stars are like pearls around a bride's throat. The roses around the wall that separates the tower from the woods are red as rubies.

There's no snow, but it's cold; I can feel it in my bones. I'm shivering, and the air mists when I huff out a breath. I'm wearing black this time, a long dress with a formal train crackling in the dry leaves when I move. I rub my arms for warmth and stare into the woods. I'm not really sure if I want to go in there. I'm thinking of wolves and witches.

I bite my lip and look behind me, back at the tower, which is warm and welcoming. I turn, making my decision. Why wander alone in the forest and get lost if I don't have to? I'd like to think that I'm more practical than the average horror-movie heroine or fairy-tale girl. It's cold and the tower is warm. End of dilemma.

I don't even know why I'm surprised anymore when a figure steps out to block my way. It's clearly a woman, but she's standing far enough away that it takes me a minute to realize she looks familiar. And she's wearing the same dress I am.

I look down at myself again, eyes widening. The train is beaded and the black black dress is long with rounded sleeves that narrow into points over my wrists under a corsage of small black roses. Strands of jet beads swing around my neck almost all the way to my waist. My hair is still rose-petal red, but it's piled up on top of my head in a fancy knot I'd never be able to duplicate.

I stare back at the woman. It's like staring at myself, only she's thinner and paler and sadder. She lifts a hand toward me and I flinch, even though I know there's no way she could touch me from over there. The gate is closed behind her. The roses are thick.

"You will never find true love," she whispers, but I can hear her clearly. "Sleep. It's safer." She steps closer, and the moonlight *falls on her face. Her eyes are my eyes. Her hair is my hair, and her mouth is my mouth.*

The wind grows colder.

She's cursing me. It's all I can think, and when she takes another step toward me, I panic and dive into the tangled briar wood. Somehow the danger of the winter woods seems kind in comparison.

I'm running as fast as I can, but I'm not covering much ground. It's hard to move between the tall thick trees since there's no path. The leaves crunch under my boots. The pine branches and hazel twigs brush against me, snagging the silk and lace of my skirt. The beads on my train pop off and glitter in the undergrowth like dark stars.

The trees sway madly in a hard wind, filling the night with their whisper. Crystals and chimes dangle from apple and aspen trees. They gleam like ice and sing like a mother's ghost murmuring a lullaby. Everything is black, the trees, the sky, me. Only the moon is bright, but I can barely see it through the knotwork of branches.

I keep running until the need for air is a cold knife in my lungs. I stumble to a stop in the middle of a small clearing circled by yew trees crowned with roses: red, white and black. I hear movement behind me, crashing between the trees. Either she's chasing me or there really are wolves in this place. Everything inside me is tight with fear. My stomach has that floating feeling, like gravity has suddenly stopped working, and my fingers are trembling. My throat is dry and the curse seems to echo in my head: You will never find true love… you will never find true love.

My mother warned me: The third dreams are always the most dangerous. I was too angry to listen. I don't know what the Shadow Lady wants from me or what she'll do to me if she finds me. Is she the type to suck bones dry or drink goblets of blood or slip me poisoned candy when I'm too hungry to care? She's already hurt me, though. I think of Poe and I want to scream.

I lean against a twisted yew trunk and close my eyes. I'm so tired. I'm just so tired. I just want to sleep and let the Shadow Lady claim me if she wants to. What does it matter anymore?

"Beauty." The voice is so soft I don't hear it at first. "Beauty." It's like a sad smile and then another voice joins it. "Beauty."

My eyes fly open. The little girl in the red dress is crouching in front of me, sulking.

"You lied to me," she pouts.

I frown at her. "Did not."

"Did too."

"Did not."

"Did too!"

I shake my head. This conversation is deteriorating rapidly. Apparently I'd had more than my share of brattiness when I was little. "How did I lie to you?"

She crosses her arms. "You said you'd protect me."

I look around. "Are you in trouble?"

She rolls her eyes. "Duh. The Shadow Lady is coming."

I scramble to my feet again, suddenly not sleepy anymore. My heart is pounding like horses' hooves in my chest. I look around frantically.

"She's not coming for you," I try to reassure the little girl. "She's coming for me."

The little girl sighs like I'm particularly slow. "I am you," she points out, stamping her tiny foot. I lift an eyebrow.

"I don't know how to stop her," I admit after a moment of charged silence. Every cell of my body is listening for the sound of footsteps. "She cursed me."

A white shadow steps out between two yews. I've never understood the cliché "jumping out of your skin" until right now. But it's not the Shadow Lady; it's my mother in her faded wedding dress.

"I can't undo the curse you placed on yourself," she says softly. "But I can give you a blessing, daughter. You may not find true love, but it will find you."

I suddenly feel like crying. I bite down hard on my lower lip to keep it from trembling. The little girl tugs sharply on my dress.

"She's coming," she says.

She doesn't have to tell me. I can feel it in the air. Everything seems to get a little darker. My mother and the little girl step away from me. I want to grab them.

"I don't know what to do!" I cry out.

"Only you can save yourself," my mother says. "No one else can do it for you." She smiles. "But I can give you a gift." She motions to a pile of leaves and then fades away, holding on to the hand of the little girl.

All I see is a pile of wet and decaying leaves. Some gift. The wind dies down and everything is suddenly still. I know the Shadow Lady is near.

Something glitters under the torn leaves and I hesitate. I tilt my head and see it again. I dig through the wet undergrowth, desperate for anything that might help. What I find is an old mirror in a tarnished elaborate frame with a handle. A lady's mirror from long ago. I hold it up and brush the mud and wet needles off it. I'm not sure how this is going to help me.

And then I don't have time to think about it anymore because there she is, standing across the clearing like a piece of midnight wearing my face. She's not doing anything, just standing there, but something about her terrifies me.

She approaches me. Panic clogs my throat. She's not making any sound this time as her feet pass over twigs and dried needles. I take a step back, but there's a tree behind me, and even if I run I know she'll find me. I haven't been able to hide from her yet.

There's something really really creepy about being stalked by someone who looks like you. The mirror's heavy in my hand. I hold it up. It must have a purpose. Why else would my mother have given it to me now? I turn it so that the glass flashes into the Shadow Lady's face. Her reflection is steady and unwavering. She shakes her head.

She's getting closer. Somehow I know that if she touches me I'll never be rid of her. I'll be numb and quiet and dead inside again, and this time I might not ever find my way out. I'll go back to sleep for a hundred years, forever.

I turn the mirror over and stare at myself.

I think of what my mother said to me, trying to find an answer to this riddle: No one can save you but yourself. And in that other dream, in the snowy courtyard: You're beautiful, don't ever forget that.

I resist the urge to look away. I remember the strength I felt just yesterday when I looked in the mirror and saw someone I could like, when I thought of myself as an artist, when Luna kissed my cheek to comfort me, and when I opened up enough to kiss Poe. That's beauty. I should open up enough to kiss myself too.

I lean closer to the glass and kiss myself on my imperfect mouth. It makes me smile. It makes the Shadow Lady smile too, even as she stops moving and comes apart like the black sky at dawn.

She wasn't cursing me after all, I think before I wake up. She was warning me.

WHEN BEAUTY WOKE THAT
Friday evening, she set to work redecorating her room. She
tore pages out of books and framed them: Millais' *Ophelia*,
Burne-Jones' *Sleeping Beauty* and Waterhouse's *La Belle
Dame Sans Merci*. She framed poems Luna had read to her
and hung them over her desk and set them up on her windowsill. She dug out all of the emergency candles her father
kept in the junk drawer in the kitchen and stuck them in
old bottles. She draped scarves over her lamps and night
tables. She spread an old quilt over her bed and hung necklaces on the posts.

Pleased, she took the rest of the candles downstairs to
the basement. She might only have one little corner, but she

would make it into her own studio. She scattered the candles about like stars and tossed pillows on the floor in one corner. She found an old blanket, painted swirling designs over it and then hung it over the back of the ancient couch. She opened one of the windows, cut an armful of roses and set them in glasses by her worktable. Outside, the cold snap dug in its heels and snow began to fall.

Inside, she painted like a woman gone mad. It filled her up and then emptied her out. She smeared acrylic paint in thick layers over a wide new canvas. She worked from memory and painted her mother asleep in her wedding dress, smiling sadly in a white bathtub set in the middle of a medieval courtyard garden. A tower rose in the distance and a forest crouched in the right-hand corner. White roses grew thick in her hair and scattered over her body. White lace foamed at her feet and on her wrists, where a single red rose grew between white buds. She brushed the thorns with silver glitter.

After a few hours, she wiped her hands and went upstairs, rubbing the back of her neck. The house was dark and quiet, but the wind was pushing fiercely at the windows. She'd heard her father come home a few hours earlier, but he hadn't said anything to her, and she'd been too caught up in her paints to care. She avoided the third step, which creaked, and slid into bed, sleeping dreamlessly.

First thing in the morning, she went straight downstairs and picked up a brush. She mixed ultramarine blue and violet, added a little white and more glitter. She opened a new tube of red paint. She mixed more colors and dotted them onto the canvas.

She painted until her fingers cramped and her shoulders were sore. She stepped back, finally, wiping a paintbrush clean, and looked over what she'd done with tired eyes. She smiled. It was far from perfect; she could probably work on the perspective and the layout, but the details were good and the moonlight glowed. It was what she'd been trying to paint for weeks now, and finally, finally, she could look at her mother and smile a little. Thaw a little.

When she went upstairs, she found a packet of needles left carelessly on the counter. Tears burned her eyes and she looked around, half-expecting to see her father. She still hadn't spoken to him, and he was at work now. She didn't know when he'd left the needles out or what he was thinking. She didn't test the liquor cabinet, didn't look in the fridge to see if the cheese was sliced or the cantaloupe cut.

Silver needles on the counter was enough.

On Sunday she dressed in a pair of jeans with a satin slip and a sweater over top. She tied her hair back in two braids and wrapped a long beaded bracelet she'd forgotten she owned around her wrist. She was finding funky clothes in the back of her closet that she'd completely forgotten about. She lined her eyes in black.

She brought her painting upstairs to dry and hoped her father would like it. She still hadn't seen him; he was doing inventory at the hardware store and probably wouldn't be home until late again. After the sun had set and she'd spent a weekend alone and actually enjoyed her own company, she bundled into her winter coat and carried a mug of hot chocolate outside.

The sudden early storm had killed the roses, shriveling them on the stems, but she didn't mind. The snow was thick and swallowed the sound and made her smile. She watched her breath fog, sipped hot cocoa and wondered if it was too cold for Poe to be out on his back porch with his guitar. At least he wouldn't know she was listening.

There was nothing but the sound of branches creaking under the weight of snow and someone shoveling out on the street. She was about to go back inside when something sailed over the fence into her yard. She didn't know what it was, but it landed in the snow. It was followed by another shape, but this one grunted when it hit the ground.

Poe stood up and looked at her, grinning goofily. Snow dusted his arms and legs like icing sugar. There was a striped scarf wrapped around his neck.

"Hi," he said.

She blinked. "Hi. What are you doing?"

"I got your e-mail."

She cringed, blushing. "Oh. I suppose it's too late to ask you not to read it and to toss your computer out the window?"

He just kept grinning. "I loved it."

"Look, I know…" She paused, tilted her head. "What?"

"You heard me."

She grinned back. "Want to come inside for some hot chocolate?"

"Sure." He dug his guitar case out of the snow and followed her inside. He sat at the kitchen table and shook snow out of his hair. She poured a cup and gave it to him, not meeting his eyes.

"You're embarrassed."

She thought of the little girl in her dream. "Duh," she said with a half-smile.

"I get embarrassed too, especially when I have to sing alone without the band." He unlatched the case and pulled out his battered acoustic guitar. He propped it on his knee and tuned it without a word.

Then he sang to her, her favorite song, soft and intimate, while the snow continued to fall from white white clouds.

⊷— EPILOGUE —⊷

SEVERAL MONTHS LATER,
when Beauty's father's fear of needles and sharp things had
mostly passed, she found herself at a tattoo parlor. It was
winter, and ice coated the streets and the sidewalks. It glittered like a painting.

She left with a small tattoo on the inside of her left
wrist— a red red rose, the same color as her hair.

Born in Montreal, Alyxandra Harvey-Fitzhenry studied creative writing and literature at York University. When not writing, she is a belly dancer and yoga practitioner. Her hobbies also include jewelery-making, art shrines and collages. Alyx lives in rural Ontario with her husband and three dogs, Medusa, a Bouvier, Yoda, a Corgi, and Hannah, a Cockapoo.

DATE DUE